2042

Artemis Rising
M.A. Mitchell

LMA

Library of Congress Control Number: 2025905109

For rights and permissions, please contact:
LMA Publishing
PO Box 105
Sunol, CA 94566

For Teresa, always

Contents

Prologue

July 2026

Sandra sensed Linda Ngo's gentle movements as she entered the room. Her parents handled the introductions, and they were left on the living room couch to talk.

"It's a pleasure to finally meet you, Sandra. Gina has spoken highly of you."

"Really? That's kind of her. Gina is a great lady, but I'm surprised she would speak highly of me to a Berkeley professor. I was a pretty average student."

"Well, it's your brain we're interested in, not your academics."

"Excuse me?"

Sandra didn't know why Linda had come to her house. If the request hadn't come from Gina Johns, Sandra would have ignored it. However, Gina was the superintendent at the California School for the Blind and a trusted friend.

"If my information is correct, you have a specific form of Optic Nerve Hypoplasia that could be relevant to our study. Can I ask you to confirm that you have no light perception whatsoever?"

"That's correct."

"Thank you. That's good."

"Umm, yeah, lucky me." This lady was already irritating Sandra, but in many ways, Sandra knew she was indeed lucky.

ONH was primarily an issue with the optic nerve, but there were often secondary brain disorders. For example, in some cases, the hypothalamus developed abnormally. That caused a lot of issues. The hypothalamus controlled the pituitary gland, which in turn controlled all of your emotions through the release of hormones. If you were happy or sad, excited or bored, frightened or content, it was your hypothalamus telling your pituitary gland to make you feel that way. Fortunately for Sandra, she had nothing more, or less, than the usual hormonal issues of an eighteen-year-old.

Linda paused and started to explain. "I'm sorry if I misspoke. What I meant is your form of ONH is a good target for our study. We're using an extremely precise form of repetitive transcranial magnetic stimulation to target the occipital lobe. Our research so far shows that we can send images directly to the brain independently of the optic nerve."

Sandra didn't know what all of that meant, but she understood enough to make her heart drop into her stomach. It was made very clear early in life that she would never be able to see. That was a fact she had accepted long ago. The psychologists called her "well-adjusted." Yet, for the first time in her life, this woman gave her the idea that she might be able to see, well, something. She probably should have been happy, but her first reaction was fear. Fear that Linda was a crackpot. Fear that her hopes would be raised and then destroyed. Fear that her life, her good life, might be destroyed by change.

Linda sensed the moment and continued cautiously. "We have been able to project low-resolution images to volunteers within the lab. What we don't know is if it will work on someone such as yourself, where that part of the brain has been dormant since birth."

Ah, here it comes, thought Sandra. The expectation setting combined with the request to be a guinea pig. She felt her fear turn into something closer to anger. *Who is this woman to come here and disrupt my life like this?* She clenched her fists into tight balls, but stayed silent as Linda continued.

"You might be wondering why we want to work with you in particular. Frankly, you fit the criteria. Specifically, someone without a functioning optic nerve yet also without any other related complications. Secondarily we want someone as young as possible so the occipital lobe will have been dormant for as short a period as possible. Yet, for legal and ethical reasons, at this stage in the research, we are required to have an adult who can give consent. An eighteen-year-old with your condition thirty minutes away from our lab makes you a prime candidate for our program."

Sandra kept her breathing deep and steady. Her hands remained in tight fists, and her lips shut.

"Speaking to Gina, there was one other reason I moved you up to the top of our list. She said you always kept a positive attitude despite adversity. Nothing seems to keep you down."

Oh, you've got to be kidding me, Sandra thought. That had to be the worst bit of pandering she'd heard in a while. It was so blatant that it made her smile despite herself. Yet that little crack of humor was all it took to allow hope to rise up again. She heard herself asking Linda about the next steps.

"We would like you to come in for some initial scans and fitting sessions. If everything looks good, we'll ask you to sign a non-disclosure agreement and contract with us. We will then create a custom headset for you at considerable expense, so we will require a twelve-month commitment to the project. We think we'll need you for an average of three days a week for four hours a day, but that's just an estimate. You are free to do whatever you'd like outside of the lab, but you must remain in the area, must not speak about the project, and must be available whenever we need you. In return, you will receive a base salary of $54,000 for the year."

Ah, okay, so this is just a job, Sandra thought. *Well, that's okay then.* She had just graduated from high school and, frankly, didn't have much else going on. She could play along with these academics and maybe take some classes at Ohlone Community College on the side. *The money sounds good, and all they want to do is mess with a part of my brain I'm not using anyway. Oh, yeah, they are messing with my brain.*

"Are you planning on irradiating my brain or something?" Sandra asked. "Will I need to take drugs or anything?"

"No, nothing like that," Linda replied. "The magnetic pulses simply trigger the brain's neurons, replicating the way they would be triggered naturally. Once you remove the headset, there's no lasting effect." Linda paused for a moment. "The main thing I want you to be aware of is that this is very much in a developmental stage. We might accidentally target the wrong neurons and send you incomplete or distorted images. Given that you have never processed visual images before, we're unsure how you'll react to some of the stimuli."

Sandra had agreed to do it before Linda had left the house. A week later, she went to UC Berkeley's Vision Research Center for the initial scans. She enrolled part-time at Ohlone. Another week went by, and she was under contract with the lab. She had her hair cut short. A month more, and they had her come in for the first real session.

She was led to a comfortable chair and asked to sit still. They placed a heavy, tight-fitting hood on her head. She could feel the weight of the attached electromagnets and wires. Sandra couldn't tell exactly how many people were in the room, but she knew Linda was there and at least a few others.

"Sandra, today will be a calibration session. We're going to send pulses to your occipital lobe. You should perceive dots or small flashes of light. We will begin in three, two, one."

Sandra let out a small yelp as she "saw" little dots of different colors flash on and off. They moved around as she perceived a field of vision for the first time in her life. Just little dots, but they were in different places, and they were . . . there. A few minutes into the session, and the nausea started. Then came a cold sweat. The field went black again.

"Sandra, we're going to give you a little break while we look at the data."

Sandra puked into her lap and onto the floor.

"We'll clean that up. How are you feeling?"

"Fine, I guess" was all she could get out as her mind was racing at what she just experienced.

"A little motion sickness is to be expected. Your body is trying to incorporate a new way of perceiving your surroundings. Those little dots probably didn't give you much of a point of reference."

Sandra didn't think it was motion sickness. Or maybe it was. But it was mostly shock. This was sight? She had no basis to compare. She literally, suddenly, had a new sense that she didn't have a moment ago.

"We can quit for the day if you'd like," Linda said, and then there was a male voice trying to quietly object to that suggestion. Sandra didn't want to quit either. She wanted to see the dots again.

A week went by, and she was back in the chair with the headset on again.

"Sandra, today we're going to try to send you an actual image. Let us know what you see."

A switch was flicked, and she heard a low hum. "Four lines . . . It's a square! No, it's four squares; two of them are one color, and the other two are a different color!"

"That's right, Sandra! The darker color is blue, and the lighter color is yellow."

And so it went for the first few months. Sandra had to learn her colors and confirm her tactile perceptions of shapes by sight. The images were simple to begin with, but slowly started to become more complex. There wasn't any more puking or cold sweats, just intense headaches by the end of each four-hour session. Yet she found herself longing to go back in between sessions. She was learning colors! She dropped out of Ohlone.

There was small talk between sessions, and Sandra got to know the other researchers. It turned out Linda was just half of the leadership team for the project. The male voice she heard arguing from time to time was Peter Graham. He was apparently responsible for the software that created the images in her head.

By month five, she was able to perceive multiple objects of various shapes against a background. She also got a sense of what people meant by "resolution," and she knew she wanted more of it.

Things started to move by month six.

"Sandra, time for something new. We're going to go from static images to images in motion." Sandra felt something being placed in her lap. "That's a bucket, in case you need it." Sandra laughed, and the room followed.

She didn't need the bucket, but the smiles didn't stop as she saw the rectangles and circles move. Peter said she was seeing "Pong," which he said was one of the first video games ever created. Seeing objects in motion felt natural to Sandra, and the end-of-session headaches started to go away.

Month seven was her next life-changing experience.

"We're going to try something different today, Sandra. Just let me know what you see when we start."

A flick of a switch, and another low hum. "I see . . . is that a person? They're sitting. They're waving an arm? It looks like there might be two other people behind the one in front. Wait, is that you waving an arm?"

"Very good, Sandra! It is indeed me. We're sending you a live feed for the first time! The image clarity still needs work, but this is the room you've been coming to for the last several months."

Maybe the image did need some work, but Sandra wept from her closed eyes as she saw her surroundings for the first time.

The non-disclosure agreement prevented Sandra from talking in detail about what was happening. However, her friends and family knew she was working in a lab, and they knew her emotions were on a roller coaster related to this work. By the time she entered the tenth month at the lab, Sandra had become unusually short and irritable at home. When her parents suggested quitting work if it made her so upset, she screamed "No!" and locked herself in her room. It was so out of character that her mom contacted Linda privately. After describing her daughter's behavior, she said that she was concerned that there may be side effects from the lab work. Linda assured her that direct side effects were highly unlikely but that they would look into it.

Sandra received a new, lighter-weight hood as she entered the eleventh month of lab work.

"We're going to do a little calibrating to start, Sandra." More dots, more blocks, more Pong, but no puking, and everything seemed a little crisper.

"Now we're going to switch over to the live feed." Suddenly, the room was revealed, and she could see like she had never seen before. She gasped in amazement as she made out some of the features on Linda's face in front of her. And there was Peter sitting there with a little smile—yes, she could see he was smiling!

"You should be seeing the equivalent of about twenty-six-thousand pixels of resolution. It's about the same as the very first digital videos on the internet," Peter said.

Sandra had no idea what he was talking about, but she was amazed by the detail that was suddenly available to her. The tears of joy started to flow. She saw Peter reach out and put an arm around Linda. *Oh, that's how it is,* Sandra thought, *nerd love!* She started giggling through the tears and then, just as quickly, started sobbing uncontrollably. Linda thought something must have gone wrong and turned off the feed, which only made Sandra cry harder.

"Sandra, are you okay? What's wrong? Have the headaches returned?"

Sandra shook her head and continued sobbing.

"What is it then? Do you want to quit for the day?"

"No! I don't want to quit."

"That's fine. Just gather yourself, and we can do some more scans to make sure everything is okay before continuing."

"You don't understand! I don't want to quit! This is my last month before the contract ends. You've shown me what I've been missing all my life, and then you're going to take it away again. It's not fair! I knew this would end badly; I just didn't know it would be this brutal!"

Through her weeping, she heard Peter and Linda pull away and murmur something to each other. Then Linda addressed her again.

"We were planning on waiting until things were a little further along to tell you, but we don't think this has to end in a month."

There it was. Hope rising again. Sandra wanted to shove it back down, but she controlled her sobbing and listened to Linda.

"We think this process, using repetitive transcranial magnetic stimulation or rTMS, to stimulate the brain has obvious commercial potential. The university has agreed to allow us to spin out our work as a private endeavor as long as we agree to pay royalties for any commercial sales.

"The potential applications go beyond restoring sight, as amazing as that is. But we will start with that as our first commercial product.

"And I know it might sound funny, but Peter has gotten used to your brain. Each one is unique, and he's gotten a sense of how yours is mapped. Having access to it going forward will help us get to market sooner. We won't be able to pay you more than minimum wage at first, but we can offer you a small amount of equity. It won't sound like a lot, just a percent of a percent, but it should grow into something if the company does what we think it might. In return, we'll need you to be in the lab full-time. When we're not actively testing, we'd like you to help out where you can. Maybe you can answer the phones for us or something?"

Sandra started crying again, but this time, they were tears of joy.

Sandra started nodding vigorously and managed to get out an "okay" in between the tears and sniffling.

And what did Linda think she would say, Sandra wondered. It was the choice between going back to being blind . . . or not.

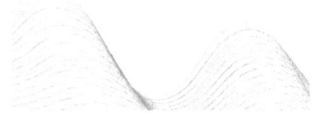

Katherine

May 2042

K atherine looked out at the peaceful waters of the San Francisco Bay far below. It was late on a sunny May morning in the City. The fog was weeks away, and the rain of winter was long gone.

Grabbing her coil from its charging cradle, she turned away from the window and collapsed on the couch. She looked up again, staring at the Bay Bridge, humming with traffic. Did her colleagues feel the same way? It wasn't something you could talk about. Peter? No, bless him. He seemed to genuinely enjoy casting. Frank? Yeah, Frank probably felt the same way she did.

The thought of work steadied her resolve. That's what this was. Work. That meant attending a cast once a month, advertising and all.

Resigned, she placed the coil on her head. A menu popped up over her vision. She navigated to the SmallNet and selected the cast she had bookmarked. "*DHF – Osprey.*"

The caster was crewing on *Osprey*, and this was the Double Handed Farallones race, which had begun a couple of hours ago. The sailing race was around Southeast Farallon Island, part of a chain of islands about twenty-four miles west of the Golden Gate Bridge. The Farallones were little known, even in the Bay Area, but Katherine remembered reading about them when she was much younger. They were nicknamed the Devil's Teeth due to their shape and the great white sharks that frequented the area.

Which was fine. Or not. Katherine didn't care. She was just fulfilling her monthly casting commitment and wanted a sailing story to tell Harbrinder.

She selected "join," and her vision dipped to black. A few seconds later, she was physically still on her couch, but also on the *Osprey*, experiencing everything through the caster. She was now a slightly younger man. They were standing with a sailboat's wheel in their hands. Their legs were stiff. A cold wind was blowing. As their eyes scanned the ocean, the waters were in stark contrast to the serenity of the Bay just a few moments before. Despite the chill, she felt sweat on their skin. Their nerves shook as the *Osprey* fell off one wave and slammed almost immediately into the next.

"I told you not to go through the Potato Patch," the caster yelled to a middle-aged man trimming the mainsail.

"My boat, my call," the other man yelled back. "Just keep the speed up and feather it right before she falls off the wave. We'll be through this before long."

Katherine wondered if she had joined a sinking ship. With each wave, the tiny sailboat felt as though it would crack in two. The caster's anxiety flowing through her body seemed to verify her concerns as the pounding continued.

"Here, let's switch places for a bit," the middle-aged man said as he moved cautiously towards the caster. Both sailors held the wheel until the *Osprey* was momentarily in the trough of a wave, then the caster moved to the bench and grabbed the mainsheet.

Katherine felt the rope in their gloved hand. They worked the mainsheet, pulling the sail slightly in and out as the *Osprey* slid up and down the waves. They scanned the horizon at the crest of each wave and could see several other sailboats to the south and, yes, behind them. A sense of satisfaction relieved some of the pain that had crept into their lower back.

They looked back at the middle-aged man at the wheel. The captain, Katherine supposed. Their eyes drifted to the sailing jacket he was wearing and focused on the HH logo on his chest. Katherine felt an artificial, but definitive, quasi-sexual feeling from seeing that label. *Ah, there it is. Fine.*

A few minutes later, the interval between waves began to increase. The *Osprey* was still taking a beating, but the pounding had turned into a roller-coaster ride instead of bumper cars.

"See," the captain said with some pride, "We're ahead of the fleet. I bet we make it around the Farallones by 1:00."

Katherine felt the caster's gratification contrast with her own feelings. She was happy not to witness a disaster, but she was done. Her lock-in period was over. She wasn't staying on the *Osprey* any longer than she had to. She clicked out and was back on the couch in her apartment. The cold, the pain, the exhaustion, all disappeared instantly from her body as it lingered in her mind.

Walking over to the kitchen, she opened the fridge, poured herself a glass of white wine, and stood at the counter, looking out once again on the tranquil waters of the Bay.

Coming to terms with the impulse bubbling up from her subconscious, she reached over and grabbed her tablet-sized glass. *Might as well get it over with.* She navigated to the Helly Hansen website and purchased her new sailing jacket.

***

The next morning the alarm clock went off at 5:45 a.m. As usual, Katherine was already awake. Swinging her legs out of bed, she began her day comfortable in the discipline of routine.

It was Monday. A work day. She had her schedule memorized, and she knew there was little chance of drama. When she was honest with herself, these average days were the ones she liked best.

She placed her slender frame into her running clothes and put her long black hair in a tight ponytail. A quick glance at her glass confirmed there was nothing urgent, so she took the elevator down to Fremont Street.

Katherine was welcomed by the start of a sunny May morning in the City. This was her favorite time of year in San Francisco. The fog was weeks away, and the rain of winter was long gone.

Slowly jogging down Mission Street, she navigated sidewalks filled with the mixed energy of people coming from late-night casts while others headed to work. The crowd was an assortment of rich and poor, young and old. Missing was the emphasis on the tech bros and the homeless from Katherine's youth. The City had finally recaptured some of its past as the cultural center of the Bay Area.

She turned toward the waterfront and felt herself gaining pace. A not-unpleasant stiffness in her legs began to loosen as her breathing became a conscious act. The scent of water, the crisp air, her heart rate increasing. She tuned in to her own body even as she became more connected to her surroundings. No earbuds, no running chip, no glass to display analytics, just the pure motion of her body through the buzz of the City.

She hit a rhythm and knew she would maintain this pace for the rest of her 3.5-mile run. She quickly passed the gathering commuters at the Ferry Terminal and began ticking off the odd-numbered piers on the north side of the Bay Bridge. Pier 1, Pier 3, Pier 5, Pier 7 . . . by the time she passed Pier 9, her mind had started to drift through the day's agenda.

Her first meeting of the day was the executive welcome at the new hire orientation. In theory, every member of the senior staff was on rotation for this assignment. In reality, her peers were good at coming up with "unavoidable conflicts," and she gave this pitch more often than any other executive. As the head of Corporate Communications, she was the obvious substitute, but Katherine truly didn't mind giving the presentation. She knew she would walk in, turn on the full "Katherine Tanaka" charm, and convert the room full of new hires into members of her growing fan club.

The thought of cultivating a fan club struck Katherine as funny. She didn't consider herself a schemer or someone who manipulated people to get ahead. She prided herself on her business ethics and behavior. She simply wasn't oblivious to her situation or how the game was played. The simple truth was that at a company the size of Artemis, with many employees doing little more than reviewing the work of AI, human beings filled the gap with politics.

Katherine looked up from her thoughts as she strode past Pier 39, empty of tourists on a Monday morning. She glanced out at Alcatraz and made the turn back toward her apartment.

Mornings like this made her happy to be back in the Bay Area. Katherine grew up in the Silicon Valley suburb of Fremont but surprised her parents by going to Penn over Stanford or Cal. After graduating with a BA in Communications in 2027, she took a PR job at a large financial services company in Philadelphia. However, it didn't take long before she grew tired of the East Coast and was looking for a role in California.

As it turned out, a small, but rapidly growing bio-tech company named Artemis was looking to hire a communications manager. Now San Francisco was home and work was Artemis headquarters on Alameda Island.

Back when she joined in 2030, Artemis had just the one building on the old Alameda Naval Air Station. Now it had not only taken over most of the station, but had transformed the entire island into "The Island." In the twelve years she'd been with the company, she'd seen the addition of a new car tunnel from West Oakland, a new terminal at the Oakland Airport, and the old Seaplane Lagoon transformed into the Bay Area's largest ferry terminal. Housing on Alameda Island itself has become some of the most expensive in the Bay Area.

Despite being a ferry ride away, Katherine originally chose to live in San Francisco because housing had become relatively inexpensive. The downtown area was still reeling from the tech exodus of the 2020s and former office buildings had gradually become apartments. Young people, artists, and the non-techie crowd were finally able to return to the City. With them came the nightlife and experiences a young woman like Katherine sought when she spared a moment from work. After all, at first she didn't know how long this job would last, so she figured she might as well live somewhere fun. Once the potential for the company had become obvious, she could have moved to the Island, but she had no desire to do so. People there lived in constant relation to Artemis. Alameda had become a company town, just like it was a Navy town until the government left in 1997. As dedicated as Katherine was to work, she also prized the separation provided by living across the Bay.

She finished her run and cooled off by walking the last block. Back up the elevator and a quick shower. The day called for a younger, but tasteful business casual outfit that a new hire might assume someone in her position would wear.

As usual, her life started to transition from personal to work over her morning breakfast. This was when she habitually reviewed the news that broke since she slept. The feed was curated by Suzi, the Comms department AI. Anything in the media that was Artemis-related and either currently trending, with the potential to grow, or flagged by another department's AI was brought to her attention. The AI certainly helped narrow the volume, but Katherine knew it was her disciplined approach to data consumption that had brought her this far. She had to be prepared if Frank, or any member of senior staff, asked her opinion on a story. Katherine had never been caught flat-footed, and she was determined to keep it that way.

Today's feed was fairly typical. The three items flagged as most likely to be discussed were:

1) Another "Could it happen here?" story related to the Second Korean War from a mid-level site. Nothing new there, and not getting much traction. Suzi recommended no action, but it might be discussed internally.

2) An opinion piece in the *New York Times* on Neo-Imperialism and Artemis's development facility in Uganda. No new content generation needed, but Suzi recommended a relatively small ad buy through a third party promoting a recent book on Africa's economic renaissance powering global GDP growth. Katherine tapped to approve.

3) A SmallNet industry group had published a report showing live stream OpenCast use had grown from two to three percent of casting over the last year. Suzi said the consensus from Artemis's own AIs put it closer to four percent. This was indeed news to Katherine as it had been hovering around two percent for years. Suzi flagged it for general awareness.

The rest of the feed was a collection of local and world news followed by a series of interview requests for senior staff that she approved or denied, largely following Suzi's recommendations.

With that, Katherine felt prepared to walk down to the ferry and head over to the Island. Most senior execs would take an AutoCab or even drive themselves. Katherine liked the ferry though. Sure, it was faster than sitting in traffic, but it was more than that. The ferry was filled almost exclusively with young Artemis employees, and she made sure they saw her as one of them. She was always willing to talk, but she was constantly amused at how few people would approach her. It was some combination of courtesy and fear that made people wary of contact.

Once on board, she headed upstairs and found a seat near the window. The ferry lurched gently into reverse and turned to the Bay. They accelerated onto hydrofoils and away from the City. Katherine had her handheld glass out and ready, but she avoided looking at it.

After all these years, the view was still worth a few moments of her time. She looked up as they passed under the original western span of the Bay Bridge, still connecting the City to Yerba Buena Island. The Golden Gate and even the newer eastern span on the Oakland side were more famous, but this part of this bridge was Katherine's. The old steel suspension bridge was a constant companion out her apartment window and the gateway to her life at Artemis. Moving clear of the towers and out into the open bay, she reviewed the easier messages of the morning while flagging the tougher ones for follow-up on campus. Ten minutes later, she saw the USS Hornet out of the corner of her eye as they entered the Seaplane Lagoon.

The Hornet was an aircraft carrier from World War 2 that was opened as a museum in 1998, a year after the Navy pulled out of Alameda. Now it had become the unofficial mascot and guardian of Artemis Corporation. As a global company, Artemis had to be careful about using overtly American patriotic symbols, but there was no ignoring having an aircraft carrier on your front door. So Artemis directed some of its local community funds toward the preservation of the Hornet. Katherine even gave a little speech at the Hornet's hundredth birthday celebration a couple of years ago. She wondered what the ghosts on board thought of a Tanaka giving a pep talk on the flight deck, but she doubted many people made the connection. A hundred years is a long time, and besides, she was as American as any of them, even if, or maybe even especially since, her grandparents spent part of their childhood in the Manzanar relocation camp during World War 2.

Secure at the dock, Katherine stepped off the ferry and walked to the AutoTram marked for Building 12. There were over thirty buildings that made up the Artemis campus, including a dedicated five-star hotel for customers and VIPs. All the buildings had their own character, but none of them were over six stories tall. Maybe it was their academic background, but Artemis's founders wanted a distributed and walkable campus rather than a mega tower. The old Naval Air Station became the ideal place to create an eccentric headquarters central to the rest of the Bay Area.

Building 12 stood out from everything else on campus. It was the largest building and clearly the nerve center of a very powerful corporation, purpose-built to house senior staff and impress visitors. Its main auditorium took up much of the ground floor. Sliding partitions opened up to create an indoor/outdoor space that could accommodate thousands during a company-wide meeting or special event. Most days, including today, it was subdivided into smaller spaces. One of those spaces housed the orientation Katherine was walking to.

"Hi, Katherine!" came the familiar voice as she walked into the lobby. It was Sandra, technically the receptionist but also a bit of a living legend at Artemis.

"Hey, Sandra, are they ready for me in there?"

"Just about. They all got back from badging a few minutes ago, and I think they're grabbing coffee inside."

"All righty then. I guess I better head in and inspire the next generation."

"Just do me a favor and leave me out of the story this time."

"Not a chance."

Katherine

K atherine surveyed the room while waiting for the program coordinator to introduce her. There were around a hundred attendees, which was typical for a new hire orientation.

Artemis had 35,000 employees in the Bay Area alone. Globally it was closer to 300,000 in fifty-four countries. The truth was the company would be more efficient with a lot fewer people. Finance and Operations estimated the right size for the company was closer to 75,000 employees, tops. But since the Collapse of 2035, keeping humans on the payroll had its benefits.

"Next we are truly fortunate to have our head of Corporate Communications provide you with a unique overview of Artemis. Katherine Tanaka has been with the company since 2030 and worked her way up through the ranks to her present position. She has seen the company evolve firsthand. I can think of no one better to be with us today. Katherine?"

"Thank you, Susan, and good morning, everyone!" Katherine started cheerfully. "Can I see a show of hands? Who knows what Artemis's first product was?" Everyone raised their hands.

"Can someone shout it out?"

A mix of shouts: "Helping the blind!" "Visual." "Medical."

"That's right. The first product helped the visually impaired community and restored sight to millions of people. Does anyone remember the name of that product line?"

Silence.

"That's okay. The name of the original product line was Tiresias. Not very catchy. But it was the name of the blind Greek Oracle of Thebes, and Peter and Linda liked that. They could see the future promise of their work. Luckily after the success of their first product, they hired some marketing people to name the rest of the products."

Polite laughter filled the space.

"Now, how many people have heard the story of Sandra Freedman, the first blind person to have their sight restored by an Artemis product?"

As usual, about half the people raised their hands.

"Good. Now, how many people know that you walked right by Sandra when you entered the building?"

A couple of people raised their hands. Also normal for that question.

"Well, let me tell you all a little bit about Sandra."

Katherine went into the story of the blind girl from Hayward who could see thanks to the products of this company. She covered the early years of refinement and how Sandra even helped them select the name of the company, Artemis, which is what she thought of whenever Peter or Linda said rTMS. More than a decade later, Sandra's "percent of a percent" of the company has made her one of the wealthiest people on the island, and yet she still worked as a receptionist "keeping an eye on her investments," as she would say. The hood and wires she used to wear to "see" were replaced by smaller and smaller headsets offering higher and higher resolution. Now a battery-powered visual-only coil could be easily hidden beneath her Hermes headband, with a pair of cameras in her Dior sunglasses providing a three-dimensional view in Ultra High Definition.

It was a fitting story to share with new hires. It covered the good the company did in the world, how it made an employee wealthy, and how, after all these years, that employee stayed loyal and humble. And it had the benefit of being true. Sandra was still a positive energy magnet and fiercely loyal to Peter and Linda. She could have retired long ago, but she seemed to honestly enjoy her job. After all, she wasn't just a receptionist—she was THE receptionist at the world's most valuable company. She regularly greeted CEOs, heads of state, and celebrities who came to Artemis HQ for one reason or another.

"Now, who can tell me when that first product, Tiresias, was approved by the FDA and made available to the public?"

"2031!" was shouted out by someone. Pretty quickly too. He might have actually known it instead of checking his glass.

"Very good! And that kicked off a series of medical advances that continue to this day."

And that was also true. As Paul and Linda correctly surmised, once they figured out how to use rTMS to activate regions of the occipital lobe, the rest of the brain would be next. The opportunity to improve the lives of millions of people was monumental.

By the time Tiresias was approved by the FDA, they had a team of five hundred working on new applications, and the company continued to double in size every six months for years. Katherine herself joined at that time to manage the external communication load that was swamping people doing the "real work."

Just a few examples of breakthroughs from the early years:

- targeting the parietal lobe could provide instant, non-addictive pain relief.

- targeting a combination of the parietal lobe and the thalamus with a link to electrodes on the limbs allowed some paraplegics to move again.

- targeting the midbrain and cerebellum allowed the completely deaf to hear.

- targeting the nucleus accumbens was used to instantly end drug addiction

- targeting the hypothalamus could relieve anxiety

Yet, a decade later, there were still some areas they had yet to crack. The piriform cortex was especially difficult to decode. It housed the only sense they had yet to address—the sense of smell. The piriform cortex also happened to be responsible for autism and epilepsy, none of which the company had been able to successfully target.

"All right then, now for the fun stuff. Who knows when the first recreational products were approved for the public?"

"2034!" from the same guy again, collecting a few sideways glances from his new coworkers.

"Yep, you got it. The first cast to the public was in 2034, right here at Artemis HQ in Alameda. Members of the press had personal coils prepared for them in advance. The looks on their faces after they experienced their first cast is something I'll never forget!"

Katherine would also never forget when she first heard about casting. It made her jaw drop when Peter and Linda explained it to her so she could explain it to the world. It was a total shift from where the company was heading. Of course, it was not called casting at first. Peter's patent submission was titled "The use of repetitive transcranial magnetic stimulation to reliably broadcast brain functionality over IP networks." It quickly got shortened to just "casting," and the name stuck once they went public.

Simply put, casting meant that you could capture what was going on in various parts of someone's brain and then send it to similar parts in someone else's brain. Not cohesive thoughts or memories, but direct experiences. Exactly what a person was seeing, hearing, touching, and feeling could be relayed to someone else. The immersion went way beyond any sort of virtual reality. You could not only transmit four of the five senses, but also, by mirroring the hypothalamus, you could duplicate the release of hormones and thus emotions. For example, if a person was suddenly frightened, you wouldn't just see, hear, and touch what frightened them, but you would actually feel as frightened as they were. And if they were just pretending to be frightened, you'd feel that too.

Katherine knew Linda would have been happy sticking with medical uses, but for Peter, this was his original goal with rTMS. He felt it was a new way to bring the world together and make people directly empathetic to each other.

The technology involved was enormously complex. You had to be able to capture and interpret what was going on in someone's brain in real-time, compress and transmit it somewhere else, then decode it and map it to the proper neurons in a different brain that had those neurons in slightly different locations.

This was not something that could be hidden under a Hermes scarf.

The receiving or audience coil was the size of a wool beanie and required an external battery pack and processor. Everything was even larger for a broadcasting coil. The basic one was the size of a snowboarding helmet. Both receiving and broadcasting coils had gotten lighter and more efficient over the years, but the form factor itself hadn't changed much. The skull simply had to be surrounded to capture or receive all that information.

Katherine continued. "At this point, the company was divided into the two main product families that we still have today. The medical side of the house and the recreational. These major product families have their sub-markets and products underneath, but both are supported by shared central corporate functions such as Supply Chain, HR, Corporate Marketing, Operations, IT, Product Security, Human Factors, and my function, Corporate Communications. The major areas of overlap are in R&D. Each product family has their own R&D budget, but there's also a central R&D group to coordinate between the product families, maintain the core OS, and take on special projects.

"Back then, a guy named Frank Kovacs was put in charge of taking the recreational products to market," Katherine said with a sly look and a smile to the audience. "You might recognize that name. Turns out that project went pretty well, and Frank became my boss, CEO of Artemis, three years ago in 2039."

"Well, I'm hoping that provides you with a good general overview of the company. I'd like to personally thank all of you for joining Artemis. I'm sure each of you will contribute amazing things to the company's future."

"Susan, if we have time, I'd love to take questions." And she meant it. She had given versions of this pitch more than a hundred times. At least there was a slight chance for something interesting in the Q&A.

"Thank you, Katherine, and yes, I think we have time for a few. Who has a question for Katherine? Let's start over here."

"Ms. Tanaka," a young woman started.

"Katherine, please."

"Okay, Katherine . . . what do you credit for your success?"

Oh boy, a suck-up question to start. Maybe this isn't going to be worth it after all. Still, she answered it honestly.

"I was lucky enough to be hired when I was, and then I didn't blow it. I didn't know how successful Artemis would be when I first arrived. But when I saw the potential, I simply didn't screw up the opportunity. I worked hard and limited mistakes. Just as simple as that."

"Okay, let's move over to the other side of the room. Yes, do you have a question for Katherine?"

"Yes," came a younger male voice. "I was wondering if you could describe the AI architecture at Artemis?"

This one was a little better. A question like that usually came from one of two sources. One, someone who really wanted to know because it was directly related to their job, and two, someone who was trying to make the pretty comms lady look stupid by asking her a technical question. She gave the guy the benefit of the doubt and assumed it was the former, but it really didn't matter. Katherine could have this conversation. The mistake people made, both men and women, was thinking the pretty comms lady couldn't possibly be technically proficient. She could have easily followed in her dad's footsteps as a computer scientist, but math was easy and boring. Humans were complicated and interesting.

AI became a buzzword while she was still in high school. She even remembered her dad complaining about it. *"It's just Machine Learning with more computing thrown at it! It's not AI! Why does everyone keep saying AI!"* And that was still true, it was still just Machine Learning, it's just that it kept maturing with more and more processing against more and more datasets and so you had really good Machine Learning compared to her dad's day. Good enough to have a major impact on almost every aspect of society. Artificial General Intelligence was still a pipe dream, but with enough computing, you could make an AI seem like it was sentient. And there was a market for that. Some people wanted their AI to have a personality. To be a friend. However, it was still just the output of human programming; there was no independent initiative, no real emotions.

She started to answer the question. "We pretty much follow the Schaer model pioneered at 3M in the early 2030s. Each department has its own AI with a discrete dataset. Parts of that dataset may or may not be limited to Artemis proprietary data depending on the department. My department, my AI, Suzi, has one of the more open datasets, as you might expect from Comms. We need to be able to pull from inside and outside of the company to make the best decisions. Sharing some data in pools with other companies helps us do that. HR is another relatively open AI except for PII, Personally Identifiable Information, of course. However, Engineering, R&D, etc., all have instances of completely closed, proprietary datasets. Operations maintain the Sovereign AI that pulls recommendations and data from all the other departmental AIs. The CEO, senior staff, and the board all have access to the Sovereign AI to inform business planning."

"Oh, thank you, Ms. Tanaka, err, Katherine," interjected the young man again, "but I just meant, what level of access do we need to give the company to our Personal AI?"

Ahh, she smiled to herself; she'd overthought this one. At the end of the day, the kid just wanted to know if he'd be tracked if he took off early on a Friday.

"The HR AI just needs standard business access for payroll and health insurance. For deeper access, including location and scheduling, different departments have their own policies on that, so you'll have to speak to your manager. Speaking for my own department, I don't need to track you on a Friday as long as you don't mind me calling with a project on a Sunday night," she said with a smile.

Susan jumped in. "I think we have time for one more. Yes, over there?"

"Katherine," started a young woman, "do you believe Artemis is making the world a better place?"

Oh boy. A sure sign of low unemployment was youth needing a reason to work beyond a paycheck. This was actually a tricky one. She had her standard answer ready, but the tricky part was not knowing if she believed it herself.

"Well, I wouldn't be here if I didn't."

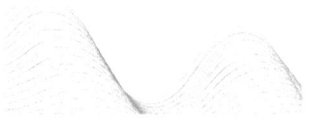

Melody

M elody couldn't help but smile and steal a glance at Sandra as she left the new hire orientation. Giving sight to the blind was a pretty cool story, but she would be working in a very different department. Her first official day wasn't until next week, so she decided to hop back on the ferry, head over to SF, and spend the afternoon continuing her apartment search.

That Katherine lady seemed okay, too. Very polished and attractive as well. Not her type, but she was sure as heck someone's type. After all, knowing someone's type was Melody's new job in a nutshell.

She would be working in the Human Factors division, which covered a lot of different aspects of the human/software interface for Artemis. She would be a lead analyst in one of the largest departments—Human Sexuality. So, yeah, basically, she would be making porn better.

She caught the AutoTram back to the ferry. The ferries ran every fifteen minutes, even in the middle of the day, so there was no real waiting. As she stepped on board, she looked around at her fellow passengers and tried to get used to the idea that these were her new coworkers. Fewer piercings and visible tattoos than back at NYU, but overall, it looked like a pretty decent cross-section of society. She wondered if she should strike up a conversation with someone. Maybe not. She wasn't quite sure how that would go.

"So what do you do at Artemis?"

"Oh, I'm working on improving mental cognition as people age by stimu-
lating certain areas of the brain. How about you?"

"I make porn better."

To be clear, she wasn't complaining. In fact, this was her dream job. She had just graduated with her Masters in Gender and Sexuality Studies from NYU and was fascinated by the space. But she discovered early on that you couldn't predict how people would react when they learned of her chosen field. Some played it cool, others thought she was a sicko, a few thought she must be a nymphomaniac. In her new professional environment, she figured she should just stick with the "Human Factors" label until she got to know people.

The truth was porn generated a lot of the early interest in casting. Artemis never promoted it, but they certainly knew it was happening. The messaging from the company—from Katherine, Melody realized—was all about the wonders of casting for education, sports, music, virtual travel, and building a connection with your fellow man. Sure, there was some of that, but it was also about sex.

Before casting, the essence of porn hadn't really changed in . . . maybe forever? Cave paintings of people having sex became watching it on a glass. That was just a change of convenience and resolution. Even with today's VR and digital sex toys, it was still just getting yourself off while watching someone else doing it. But with casting, you were the one having sex. It was totally different and also very, very complicated.

Human Factors was quickly formed to understand the space and allow for safe use without it getting out of hand. The rumor was Peter, the primary inventor of casting, was no prude, but also never intended to be the smut king of a new age.

Peter directed the Human Factors team to partner with academic researchers to understand this brave new world. Academics, including those at NYU, were more than happy to engage as casting was a treasure trove of information. The data set for neuroscience jumped from hundreds of subjects in a lab to millions of people participating in real activities while having their brains actively scanned by an Artemis broadcasting coil. And a lot of those activities were sexual in nature. The rapid academic advancements that followed were a major part of the curricula for NYU Master's program, and now Melody was joining the company that made it all possible. Yep, dream job.

Casting signals from one brain to another meant having detailed mappings of both brains to account for differences. All brains are slightly different, but gender plays a huge role in how your brain is built. For example, women tended to have a larger hippocampus, while men tended to have a larger amygdala. For most of the signal, it was just a matter of mapping like to like. It required processing a lot of data very quickly, but it was straightforward. However, in some cases, the differences were profound, and transcoding was required. In other words, if you didn't have a match, you tickled a slightly different neural circuit than the one the broadcaster was using. The need to transcode was most common when the broadcaster and the receiver were different genders. For the end-user, transcoding could make the cast feel synthetic, depending on the amount required.

Which neural circuit to target, in what circumstance, on what sort of brain structure was as much art as science in the beginning. The ongoing refinement of the decision tree for transcoding was going to be part of Melody's role. For example, if a man was receiving a cast of a woman having sex, so he was effectively experiencing the role of the woman, which neural networks did you target on the man? And what if the man was gay and the woman was heterosexual? What if the person receiving the cast was transgender? To complicate things further, what the data quickly showed was that no one was a hundred percent male or female, gay or straight, at least as far as our brains were concerned.

Artemis didn't directly create porn any more than it created other content. Most of it was on the SmallNet. What Artemis did do was provide the industry with a robust set of personas that allowed them to tag content appropriately. It was in everyone's interest for users to find the casts they wanted. The better you tagged your content, the more likely you were to have high ratings. Mistagging, even accidentally, could kill a content provider's revenue stream. For example, if Jack was fantasizing about hooking up with red-headed Trixie and suddenly found himself on the receiving end of brown-haired Mark, he may be upset. Melody would be helping to maintain those personas.

The porn industry itself transformed dramatically, and Melody thought, for the better. It could no longer be two (or more) attractive people going through the motions, pretending to be excited. The person wearing the broadcasting coil, at least, had to be really enjoying things, or the broadcast was a failure. Amateurs became the new stars, at least until they, too, got bored. Fakers were relegated to the internet.

So she wouldn't be helping the blind to see or the deaf to hear, but she was proud of the work she would be doing. She strongly felt the appropriate use of casting for sexual activity had been a positive for society. Sexual assaults had dropped steadily since casting was introduced. Violent rape was almost unheard of in the United States by 2040. Unaddressed sexual frustration that led to illicit behavior was just extremely rare.

Even better, Artemis's morals seemed to align with Melody's own, which made the job that much easier. In short, consenting adults should be able to do what they want as long as it doesn't involve violence or minors. Any content that broke the rules was aggressively policed by the company. Unfortunately, there was still some unsavory use on the OpenNet, but she wouldn't be anywhere near that.

Melody was suddenly jolted from her thoughts as the ferry veered to the side and blew its horn five times. She looked up as they passed within twenty feet of a sailboat, sending it rocking in their wake. Some guy on the sailboat was flipping off the ferry as they went by. She smiled to herself. *Hey, a little bit of New York right here in the Bay.* She was looking forward to her new commute.

Harbrinder

Harbrinder flipped off the ferry captain as he blew the five-horn warning. *Idiot.* With their autopilot handling most of the navigation, these "captains" were like children who got to push the horn button if they were good little boys and girls.

Well, maybe he did tack in front of the ferry, but it was impossible to stay completely clear with so much high-speed traffic between Alameda and San Francisco. Captain Hornblower was probably just staring at his glass until he looked up and scared himself.

Harbrinder took a deep breath. He came out here to relax. He was reaching along the City front now, feeling the wind in the sails and the smooth movement through the water of his forty-two-foot sailboat, *Blackfish*. Life wasn't so bad, was it?

Blackfish was his one true love (sorry, Katherine). He had her commissioned in Sausalito shortly after getting his MBA. Her hull was cold-molded wood that gave her a traditional look while being stronger and lighter than fiberglass. She had the long overhanging lines and counter stern of a classic wooden racing yacht. The mast and boom were carbon-fiber with a faux wooden finish to maintain the vintage look. All the rigging was high-strength synthetic fiber. Photovoltaic inlays on the wood decking kept her batteries charged. Her autonomous systems were all world-class. She had real-time telemetry sensors in the hull and woven into the sails. The autopilot used that data to automatically trim the sails using two-way electronic winches. She could navigate herself through just about any situation using AIS, GPS, radar, and sonar. Her onboard satellite networking was pretty common these days. A little more unusual was the corporate-level EM sniffer and shield, ensuring no electronic signals left *Blackfish* without his approval. All designed to make it easy for him to take her out by himself whenever he wanted or to simply work on board in complete privacy. At the moment though, he had all that automation turned off. A big part of the joy of sailing for him was the actual sailing part, and *Blackfish* was a pleasure to helm.

Harbrinder grew up as an only child in Palo Alto. He was a good kid, but his teachers called him distant or even cold. He never had, nor felt he needed, close friends his age. He simply didn't care. His family was enough, or more specifically, his father. Yet he saw his dad's concern when he didn't behave the way the other kids did. So, even if he didn't actually feel it, he listened when he was told how he should feel and act. He especially liked the rules about right and wrong. It not only told him how to conduct himself, but it also made logical sense. It was how the world should work.

His dad had been a big shot at Google back when the internet was still dominant. Beyond family and technology, his father was passionate about animals and sailing. The Singh Animal Shelters in Redwood City and San Leandro became what the family was locally renowned for. Less famously, the sailing took the form of a small J Boat they would race, poorly, from time to time. Yet the sailing stuck with Harbrinder and the animal shelters less so, although he still used the saving puppies and kittens angle when it suited him. Eventually, a degree in Computer Science from Cal Poly and an MBA from Stanford set him up to take a chunk of Dad's money over to Sand Hill Road as a junior VC. He did okay. The money made money. But over time, he started to see something in technology, and especially in digital media, that he couldn't quite shake.

He had grown up thinking technology was usually good and was generally moving human beings forward. His dad encouraged this train of thought, and Harbrinder's lifestyle had obviously benefited from this belief in technology, so who could argue? When he was a little boy, his dad loved to show him Google's Code of Conduct, which famously said, "Don't be evil."

Yet after he had grown up and started working in the industry, it became increasingly clear to him that any digital media company needed to manipulate its user base to be relevant or even just to survive. That manipulation would be packaged in a lot of different forms, some worse than others, but at the end of the day, serving the audience had to be secondary to using the audience. The days of a simple transaction—"I pay you, and I get this. If I like it, I will keep paying you"—were long over. You had to manipulate users to keep them clicking, you had to sell the data, you had to feed them ads, and those ads had to make them buy. Failure to do some combination of these things meant going out of business. Those who did do these things would eventually outgrow and outspend the competition. Frustratingly, end-users didn't seem to care. The data suggested users actually preferred being manipulated as long as they felt catered to.

The damage to society was well-documented and hardly debated, but generally ignored. Bubbles of personal preference were continuously exaggerated by new media companies for profit. It was a standard formula to keep users clicking. Stay in your bubble and occasionally be shocked by something outside of it. Rinse and repeat.

The bubbles could be political, national, racial, or socio-economic. Usually, the algorithms catered to a combination of multiple pre-existing prejudices to maximize engagement. The victims ranged from teenage girls thinking they weren't pretty enough, to the poor desperate to be rich, to the middle-aged man convinced that his country had turned against him. All dividing people against each other and against themselves. All to make a handful of people wealthy.

It got so he would sit and listen to a start-up pitch from the latest social media idea, and he would ask them to just cut to the point where they would manipulate users. And they all had an answer ready. It was always part of the business model. It was packaged in nice terms, like "leveraging the user base," but at the end of the day, it was about manipulation.

Bringing up his concerns to his colleagues only made him more frustrated. They treated him like an idiot, not because he was wrong, but because he acted like he'd made some big discovery. Of course, media companies had to manipulate their users! What was wrong with that? They provided a service, and they had to be profitable. People could just click somewhere else if they didn't like it! But they couldn't click somewhere else if all the companies were doing it; the only choice was which one of a handful of companies you wanted to be manipulated by. This was not technology serving humanity. This was a few people using technology to serve themselves.

It went against everything Harbrinder had been taught. He became so upset that he started shifting the family money toward projects attempting to break the cycle. He became a heavy supporter of community-run, open-source concepts, such as OpenID, which preserved privacy and made it more difficult for companies to monetize user data. It felt right. Wasn't this how his dad described the early days of the internet?

However, none of the projects were making any money, and it didn't look like they ever would. Spending millions to grow a large user base that you refused to "leverage" was a dead end financially. In fact, it got so bad that his dad pulled the plug on him in 2033. Oh, Harbrinder was still very comfortable, his dad got involved before it got too out of hand, but he no longer had access to a big chunk of the family fortune and, by extension, the VC industry.

In retrospect, he realized why his dad had stopped talking about "Don't be evil" when Harbrinder was in college. Google dropped it from its Code of Conduct in 2018. They stopped being hypocrites.

In the years that passed since he got kicked out of the VC world, he watched Artemis take over the media landscape. His worst fears had come true. Here, you had one company, a monopoly with no real alternative, with an insanely powerful advertising engine that could manipulate its users any way it chose. No one was going to just give up casting once they tried it, and the advertising was so effective that it was regulated by the FDA, the FCC, and, since 2040, the World Casting Association.

And all of this was why Harbrinder needed to blow off some steam sailing on a Tuesday afternoon. His dad, bless his soul, had passed on in 2036, a year after his mother, and so Harbrinder once more had control of real money. He started using that money again, but this time to take on the new Goliath of the industry. He had been working hard on "The Project."

Artemis had largely been able to maintain a monopoly on casting since the introduction of its first products in 2034. The patents certainly helped, but what really locked them into their current position was being both first to market and first to scale. In order to either broadcast or receive a cast, you had to have a custom coil made for your particular brain. Artemis provided the tools to perform the scans to medical practitioners at cost. The scans were then sent back to Artemis. A customer from that time forward could order their coil directly from Artemis with whatever options they desired. In addition to this, Artemis regularly sent out software updates to "ensure the safety and security of their products." Coils whose software was too far out of date would no longer function.

Any competitors would have to get their headsets approved by the FDA, convince medical practitioners to use their system, and give customers a reason to bother switching when all the content was on the Artemis SmallNet and BigNet. No one in the US bothered to try. There was no big push for change from the general public. Wasn't it easier if we were all just on one system?

A small sliver of hope opened up in 2037 when the Supreme Court ruled that Artemis's brain scans were covered by HIPAA. In other words, brain scans were part of your personal medical record. This meant that anyone who requested it could get a copy of their own brain scan thirty days after requesting it in writing. You could theoretically take that scan to someone besides Artemis and ask for a coil. The problem was, that coil wouldn't work with Artemis broadcasting without the proper software.

So there was still no market alternative. However, Artemis brain scans became a rallying point for the open-source community. Backward-engineered standards and software began to emerge for both broadcasting and receiving. Kits started to become available that allowed people with enough technical chops to build coils based on Artemis brain scans and open-source software. The OpenCast Project emerged.

Using homemade electromagnetic coils on your head with limited security systems and community-built fail-safes had a very limited audience, but it became possible to cast without Artemis.

Outside of the US, it was a slightly different story. Artemis was dominant globally but banned in several countries. The largest of these countries is China, which has had its own version of casting since 2037, called the People's Network. It was a knock-off of this platform that caused all the problems in Korea.

Even with its globally dominant position, Artemis still had to conform to the rules and regulations of every country it operated within. In the United States, that was mostly the FDA and the FCC. The main constraints involved the type of content allowed, what could be advertised, and the strength of synthetic reactions to a product or concept that could be introduced. For example, almost every country banned alcohol ads over casting. No one wanted to create a nation of alcoholics. Advertising for junk food was generally allowed, but the strength of the enticement permitted varied from country to country. Many, but not all, countries banned political advertising. It was complicated enough within a country, but on top of it all, there were rules around casting between countries that varied depending on which countries were involved. Want to watch a US-based cast in the UK? What about in Dubai?

Needless to say, there was a large team of people working within Artemis to manage all the different rules by country and between countries. Human Factors, Product Security, the Engineering teams were all involved, in addition to Government Relations, a division of Corporate Communications under the lovely Katherine Tanaka.

The charter for the World Casting Association was to develop common global standards for these rules. Artemis was all for the creation of the WCA since it promised to simplify its job of managing a hodgepodge of regulations in different countries. They also hoped it would help defer concerns that another incident like Korea could occur. For Harbrinder, it just meant that the few who were manipulating the many had become more efficient.

By now, The Project, as Harbrinder called it, was what he spent almost all of his time on. His goal was to break the Artemis monopoly and turn casting over to the public. His tool was the network of open-source non-profits and third-party companies that made up the OpenCast Project. He wasn't overt about his involvement, and his name was never at the top of any one organization. The average OpenCast user had never even heard of Harbrinder Singh. Yet he felt he was a godfather to the OpenCast community. The top devs knew they could contact him if they needed funding for R&D or to keep a critical component of the OpenCast network functioning. Through subsidiaries, he held a majority stake in most of the small companies trying to stay afloat in the open-source casting world. In a lot of ways, it took Harbrinder back to his VC days. If he liked a pitch, he would fund it and try to guide it remotely as a mentor. If not, he would tell them why it fell short. He felt it was the most important work of his life, but also the most consuming.

Harbrinder cleared the edge of the City, put a reef in the mainsail, and entered the Slot. This part of the Bay was a playground for sailors, created by Mother Nature's own vacuum. As the air in the Central Valley heated and rose, it created a pressure gradient that tried to suck in the cooler marine air from the Pacific. The coastal range blocked most of the cooler air from coming inland at sea level. However, there was one little opening along all those hills, the Golden Gate. The wind seemed desperate to take advantage of the opportunity and charged through the Gate most afternoons from early Spring to the middle of Fall, creating what sailors called "The Slot."

Blackfish heeled over and raced ahead as she caught the wind. Harbrinder looked over to the Golden Gate Bridge and tried to imagine how it might look if the Golden Gate Locks proposal became a reality. They said the Locks wouldn't change the sailing too much. They would only be five feet out of the water at high tide. High enough to block the sea but not the wind.

Sea levels had risen about a foot over the last fifty years. In some parts of the world, the impact, combined with seasonal storms, was catastrophic. So far, the Bay Area had only seen an increase in nuisance flooding during the highest tides. So far. The problem was the next foot of sea level, and the one after that, were already baked in. The world had changed the way it had lived, but the damage was done. The global rise in living standards combined with centuries of abuse would continue to take its toll. Still, he had to admit seeing the Locks under construction would be an impressive sight. Two massive sets of moveable reinforced gates on either side of the Golden Gate Bridge that could be closed during King Tides or a storm surge to effectively seal off the Bay from the Pacific Ocean. When the gates were shut, the Bay would technically become a lake. The upstream work would be even more impressive than the Locks themselves. Further up the Sacramento River, the diversionary reservoirs, wetlands, and flood gates around Grizzly Bay would need to temporarily stem the Sacramento's flow. On average, the Sacramento River discharged 23,500 cubic feet of water every second, so the coordination between the Locks and the diversionary systems was critical. Still, they would only need to hold back the river for a few hours at a time and then only during the highest of tides. All that effort to save billions of dollars of Bay Area real estate from flooding, including parts of the Artemis campus.

Harbrinder watched as a huge container ship came in under the Golden Gate Bridge, on its way to unload and refuel from the hydrogen farm at the Port of Oakland. A ship that size couldn't even make it under the bridge at high tide. He remembered being in awe as they sailed past similar ships in the little family sailboat. He loved them until his dad told him that container ships burned the cheapest, dirtiest type of diesel fuel. A single one of them released as much greenhouse gas in its lifespan as thirty million cars. Those days of dirty ships were gone, but the carbon remained.

Harbrinder turned *Blackfish* downwind into Raccoon Strait, her thin lines cutting into the current rushing by Richardson Bay and out the Gate. He gave a glance to the Corinthian Yacht Club, still there after all these years, and drifted past Ayala Cove. He gybed toward Bluff Point and gave the one-fingered salute to Peter and Linda's house on the hill. The two richest people in the world, living on a fourteen-acre estate on the Tiburon Peninsula, paid for by Artemis. He gybed back and rounded Angel Island by the old immigration station center and entered the Island's wind shadow. From here, he could see the hydrogen refinery in Point Richmond. Hydrogen was produced by splitting water from the brackish inner bay. A dedicated microreactor provided the heat and electricity needed. The resulting gas was piped to the Port of Oakland and beyond. Once the wind had completely died, he switched on *Blackfish*'s electric motor to keep moving and reduced sail before reentering the winds of the Slot. Within a few hundred yards, he would go from no wind to too much wind. He could tell from the whitecaps and the heeling sailboats ahead that it was blowing twenty-five to thirty knots, not unusual and a lot of fun on the *Blackfish*.

Once past the Slot, he entered the relative calm of the lee side of Treasure Island, slipped under the Bay Bridge, and on past Yerba Buena Island.

He felt restored by the sail as he motored once again down the Oakland Estuary back to Jack London Square. He had a few hours before meeting Katherine for dinner. Enough time to shower on board and get a little work in.

Jeff

J eff had been snowboarding hard all winter long. He'd dream about it at night and hit the slopes whenever he could. Getting outside in the crisp air and shredding the mountain was so addicting. He tried to limit himself to once or twice a week, but man, it was hard. He was mastering all the best freestyle runs down Mammoth just as the season was ending. Ended up with a couple of T-shirts made from recycled fibers to remember it by.

As the season ended, he had found kite foiling as a replacement. He'd do a wing foil as well, but there was something about the power of the kite, slicing through the Slot at twenty knots past all the slow sailboats. Sometimes he wouldn't even do the Bay. Last week, it was the North Shore in Maui. Totally different scene. More relaxing, less intense. Both featured plenty of sustainable seafood ads.

Of course, he had to limit himself because of the money. Even though his profile was verified as low-income, the ads would still drive him to use up what little money his parents gave him. Getting away from those ads was the main reason he spent all his Christmas money on an OpenCast coil. The OpenNet was cool in spots, but he would still end up on the SmallNet multiple times a week. The very best casts were always there. You couldn't even find snowboarding or kite foiling on the OpenNet because their broadcast coils weren't waterproof. Only Artemis had enough users to justify those kinds of custom coils.

Still, he did find some good casters to follow on the OpenNet and spent most of his time there these days to avoid the ads. He made sure they were all well-known casters. You did not want to go wandering around on the OpenNet. If you went off the map, there be monsters. All the tags were not to be trusted, and the persona matching was weak at best.

There was one guy on the OpenNet he had been following since January. He was a chef in a busy upscale Ramen place in Manhattan. His coworkers would tease him about wearing a broadcast coil all shift long, but the guy had his followers. He worked long hours, so Jeff would just tune in whenever and enjoy the flow of the restaurant. The dinner rush was satisfying, but he enjoyed the quieter moments the best, just chatting with coworkers he had grown to care for over the years. He loved all the little bits of local gossip and to hear about life in New York. There were times he would stay on all the way from the start of the shift until closing. Maybe someday he would go there himself and eat at that restaurant. He wondered what it would smell like.

So yeah, no kite foiling on the OpenNet, but it was pretty cool just to tune in to someone all day without having to worry about the ad jones afterward.

Jeff's parents got on him about joining casts all the time and not working, but he was just twenty-one. They didn't understand that this was what people did now. They were so old-fashioned that they didn't even let him get a coil until he was eighteen. In his mind, he felt he was just playing catch up on all the good casting he had missed. He knew it was good to work, but he also didn't see much of a reason. He wasn't a great student in high school, and there wasn't anything he was particularly good at. He had a few friends running around trying to get ahead, but what was the point? His parents had a place for him to live, and damn, casting lives seemed as good as any life he would ever live.

He was joining a growing legion of "castaways," and that was just fine by him. You got to experience so much more than people just stuck in their day-to-day. He knew he could stop whenever he wanted to, and when he did, he bet he would know a thing or two more than those who didn't have all these different moments.

Sure, Jeff didn't have a girlfriend, and technically he was still a virgin, but he was hardly uninitiated. He'd had dozens of women on the SmallNet, just had to pay the ad price. That had to be cheaper than a girlfriend anyway. He just wished they didn't advertise veggie-based meat on those casts so much. A couple of years with a coil, and he had almost become a damn vegetarian. Still, he wasn't going to wander off into the OpenNet for that kind of content. Click on the tags for "hot MILF rocks young apprentice," and you ended up tied down in an Uzbeki prison cell, having your testicles electrocuted. No, thank you.

So, yeah, he was a castaway, but who was to argue it wasn't a good life for him to live?

The only downsides seemed to be occasional trouble sleeping and maybe getting a little out of shape. He would work on that. Maybe walk around the block in the morning. He could do that while his coil was charging.

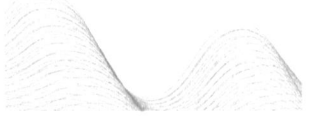

Frank

F rank Kovacs looked out the window as the Airbus 424 rose from the Oakland International Airport. Artemis headquarters was directly below and hidden from view, but he could just catch a glimpse of the sailboats in the Oakland Estuary. It looked nice down there. Floating along. Certainly better than his next thirty-six hours spent on four different planes trying to get to Uganda. Business travel just wasn't like it used to be, not that traveling to Kampala from the United States had ever been quick and easy. Still, if he was the CEO of a company like Artemis twenty years ago, it would have involved flying private for at least part of the trip. Those days were long gone now. First, the CO_2 emissions from private jets became unfashionable and bad press, so most company boards stopped approving them. Then in 2028, the EU banned the sale of carbon-based jet fuel for private or commercial use in EU airspace by 2035. Good for the environment, certainly, but a more cynical view would point out that Airbus was way ahead of Boeing in low-emission flight and stood to get a lot of business. Regardless, the new regulations spawned a commercial aircraft transformation similar to the overhaul of the automobile industry in the 2020s.

Battery-powered multi-rotor flight became the standard for making trips under two hundred miles, essentially replacing the internal combustion helicopter. Peter and Linda had a nice little model that they used to get from Tiburon to Artemis when needed. However, hydrogen, not batteries, ended up being the new fuel source for anything larger, going further. In long-range commercial aircraft, it was burnt in place of carbon-based jet fuel to power turbojets. No fuel cells. Just straight-up combustion without the CO2. There was still a little NOx, but nothing like the original jets.

It wasn't just a matter of bolting new engines onto existing aircraft. Everything had to be redesigned from the ground up. Hydrogen was much less energy-dense than carbon-based fuels, so more of the aircraft was devoted to fuel. Planes became lighter, with longer wingspans, carrying more fuel and fewer passengers. Even with all the new designs, flights over three-thousand miles were rare. You could no longer make it from San Francisco to Tokyo in one hop.

Frank's trip to Uganda would mean flying to New York, then to Heathrow, next to Cairo, and finally to Kampala. What a pain in the ass. Still, it had to be done, and at least the first two legs would be on new Airbus 424 executive class flights. The airline industry realized they could tap into the VIP demand that was left unserved by the death of the private jet. The standard 424 could hold 120 passengers in a mix of business and economy class. However, the executive class versions held just forty passengers and were a hundred percent first class. They departed from the old private jet hangers with a separate security process from the masses. At least for this portion of the trip, Frank had his own little cabin to sleep, eat, and work. Privilege still had its privileges.

Then again, twenty years ago someone like him probably wouldn't be going to Uganda in the first place. Now he tried to make the journey at least once a year. After all, he was Artemis's chief salesperson. In this case, he'd be selling the idea that Artemis cared about Uganda. Yes, he always had to sell that idea to the Ugandan people and leadership, but they weren't really an issue. His main targets were the people claiming Artemis abused the Ugandan people and supported a brutal dictatorship. Frank thought these critics were short-sighted and naive. He'd already seen the positive changes in the country since they first set up shop in Kampala six years ago. Not only was the standard of living rising, but the government was beginning to loosen restrictions and trust its own people. The country had started moving from fear and oppression to hope and prosperity. He also knew that Peter was personally pushing for the Ugandan government to decriminalize homosexuality, something that was only possible due to Artemis's pull in the country.

Not that Uganda was a paradise. He had to admit that when Linda came to him with the idea of an African R&D center, his first choice was in neighboring Kenya. Working with people like the Maasai in a stable democracy sounded pretty incredible. Unfortunately, the Kenyan government had too many regulations and remained wary of the company. Neighboring Uganda was much more willing to provide what the company was looking for. That is to say, an equally diverse population and a friendly legal environment.

When she first brought up the idea, Frank thought Linda's concept was brilliant. The company had already been growing at a monumental pace, yet there was even more opportunity to expand in both the medical and recreational space. Rapidly testing across a genetically diverse population was one of the bottlenecks to that growth. The United States was fairly diverse, at least compared to other Western countries, but the legal framework slowed everything to a snail's pace. To harm a patient, even one who had volunteered and signed all the right paperwork, could kill a project. Not to mention the bad press for the company.

Besides, if you really wanted genetic diversity, Africa was the place to be. Some people confused racial or cultural diversity with genetic diversity. In other words, manufactured social diversity instead of true biological diversity. Yet when you looked at the human genome, skin color was an insignificant part of the whole and had nothing to do with brain structure. The truth was the birthplace of humanity still maintained its storehouse of genetic diversity. And of all the places in Africa for diversity, Uganda was near the top of the list. Combine that with a strong central government that could provide Artemis with an environment to work freely, and you had a winning combination. Testing could be done quickly, and if there was an accident, the volunteer, or their surviving family, would be reasonably compensated.

What the critics didn't seem to understand is that Artemis had a huge backlog of Ugandans wanting to participate in testing. Many more than they could accommodate. On the recreational side, it was an opportunity to make good money while doing nothing more than sitting and experiencing things. Rarely, there might be some mental trauma involved, but the most common side effect was a week-long craving for a product you'd never have. On the medical side, it was riskier, but the money was even better.

The impact to the world was that casting became safer, more ailments could be addressed by rTMS, and Uganda was slowly progressing as a nation. Yes, a handful of people suffered to make it possible, but it was nothing compared to the mining industries in neighboring countries or the industrial accidents of the past. Nevertheless, he was off to spend some time in Uganda to show he cared.

Frank stretched out his legs and brought out his glass to get some work done. Maybe he was showing his age, but he still preferred to use a large glass and keyboard to work. He got into the habit of using a laptop in his early years at Genentech back in the 2020s. Then in the 2030s, the total ubiquity of network connectivity finally killed the concept of separate computing devices. It became cheaper and easier to offer centralized, cloud-based services on whatever compatible display or input device that you wanted to interact with. In other words, a piece of "glass." Old tech companies like Apple or Google charged you for the UI service, and then a whole host of third parties created input devices with biometric authentication that were more or less commodities. Frank mostly stuck with a larger glass/keyboard combination and a smaller one that reminded him of a phone from his younger days. Some folks preferred a wearable device or actual glasses, but old habits died hard for Frank.

He queried Caesar, the Sovereign AI, for recommendations on what he should focus on. Caesar suggested three tasks:

- *Catch up on personal responses to messages from extended staff.*

Frank let assistants, digital or human, handle most messaging. However, a response from the boss himself always helped team cohesion.

- *Raj Patel's hardware team has missed a development deadline for the next-generation broadcasting coil. Suggest reviewing the data and asking for a formal in-person project debrief while in India, the next stop after Uganda.*

- *OpenCast use has grown to an estimated 4% of all casting over the last year. Suggest developing a containment strategy to limit further expansion.*

Okay, that last one is interesting. Frank could never understand how OpenCast had any use at all, much less a four percent market share. *I mean, honestly, who is using this stuff?* He had a hard time believing that anyone hated Artemis so much that they would risk using a system with unverified tags and limited fail-safes.

Artemis essentially had a monopoly on casting in almost every country it operated within. Frank had had several very blunt conversations with Peter and Linda about their own "rules" regarding protecting that monopoly. Essentially, they wanted to maintain monopolies if they believed it was in the best interest of society. What this translated to in practice was a relatively lax policy on the medical side and a very strict one on the casting side.

There were a number of different companies all around the world using rTMS in the medical industry. Artemis was still the largest, but there was no way they could go after all possible applications in a reasonable time frame. So Peter and Linda felt it was best to only enforce patents when they already had a proven application in market.

On the casting side, it was a whole different ball game. They all agreed that it was in the public's best interest to have one delivery system for casting. It allowed for safe interoperability, fail-safes aligned to personal tolerances, and the appropriate use of synthetic experiences such as advertising. Besides, this was Frank's original baby, and he was protective of it. He brought recreational casting to market in 2034, used that to move up to COO starting in 2036 and then to CEO in 2039 when Peter and Linda stepped back from daily operations.

Frank knew casting would be a goldmine from the start. The key was to structure the offering to remain unique and highly profitable for as long as possible. Luckily, he had decades of watching tech monopolies rise and fall before he designed the casting ecosystem.

Peter and Frank agreed that Artemis would always control both the hardware and software but would use third parties for both content and services such as the initial brain scans. Where they differed, at least initially, was in the use of advertising as an additional revenue source. Peter was against the idea and wanted to go with an ad-free subscription model. Frank thought this was short-sighted. The ad model had three huge benefits. First, it subsidized the cost of the headsets, getting casting into the hands of more people, sooner. Second, it allowed Artemis to pay content providers, both on the SmallNet and on the BigNet for the casting of professional sports and entertainment. Finally, it provided an ongoing revenue stream for years to come.

In the end, Peter agreed to a compromise after a series of pre-launch meetings with US regulators on how casting would be governed. The compromise allowed for a high-end, ad-free subscription model and a low-cost ad model. Several years later, only about twenty-five percent of the casting audience globally were willing to pay an average of $400 per month to be ad-free. As Frank predicted, most users chose the low-cost option and advertising was now Artemis's number one revenue stream.

Casting discussions with various governments around the world were always interesting. The launch in the US provided a model to replicate in most places, but each country wanted to have its own rules, especially around some of Artemis's deeper embeds. The World Casting Association would hopefully centralize a lot of that. Having a primary governing agency would make things easier for Artemis, just like having only one system to govern made things easier for countries around the world. Governments were slow to break up the Artemis monopoly since having one throat to choke was easier. And that was probably the key to stemming the growth of the OpenNet. While some countries may have wanted an alternative to Artemis, none of them wanted an unregulated system. He decided to ping Katherine.

"Quick call?"

"Sure, one sec."

Katherine's face popped up on his glass.

"Hey, boss. Ah, on your way to Uganda, I see. First leg?"

"Yeah, brutal, but at least I can get caught up on a few things. Have you seen the latest OpenCast report?"

"Yeah, that was interesting. Industry sources say up to three percent, and internal sources say closer to four percent," Katherine said.

"Yep, that's it. I think we should be prepared to cover it in the next WCA meeting. Can you have it added to the agenda of the Ethics Committee?"

"I probably can. I'll also reach out to Human Factors to see if they know what's driving the uptick."

"Great, thanks, Kate. Let me know when it's confirmed, will you?"

"Will do," Katherine said. "Anything else?"

"Nope, that's it for now."

"All right, safe travels, and ping me as needed."

"Will do."

Frank ended the call, slipped off his shoes, and started looking into why the hell Patel kept missing deadlines.

Katherine & Harbrinder

After Frank ended the call, Katherine put down a reminder to talk to Peter about adding OpenCast to the Ethics agenda at the WCA. Peter gave Frank a great deal of freedom in running the business of Artemis, but Ethics was Peter's pet project. She wouldn't move forward without his blessing. Still, it was interesting to see Frank was serious about stemming OpenCast.

In general, she hated acting like a glorified event planner, but the World Casting Association meeting was different. She was glad Frank contacted her directly, especially for anything related to Ethics. Artemis was hosting the meeting, and its image was very much on the line. The government bureaucrats that would be descending on Alameda were some of the most powerful people that nobody had ever heard of. They would literally be deciding what people would see, hear, and feel in the future.

Katherine sent a note to her peer in Human Factors to see if they could look into what was driving users to switch to OpenCast, then she stretched, got up, and looked out the window on the top floor of Building 12. It was getting late, but she had one more meeting to go. The sun had moved to the west behind the Bay Bridge and the City. The light played across the water, and a fleeting moment of contentment washed over her. Then it was gone. With a sigh, she turned back to her desk and connected to her extended staff meeting for Asia + ANZ.

On her large glass, she could see the early morning sunshine behind some of the participants, others were still in the dark. "How is everyone doing this morning?" Katherine said.

There was a chorus of responses from the mix of faces representing several countries and departments from across the region. Some of these people she liked, some she tolerated, but they were all on this call for a reason.

"Okay, let's get started. I have everyone's new headcount targets that I'd like to share, but I don't want to hear any complaints. I expect everyone to meet their targets."

She knew her team wouldn't like it, but they needed to hire more people. She was starting to fall behind her peers in the region. Nobody enjoyed having to create work for people, but that's the way it'd been since the Collapse. Especially for a company as profitable as Artemis and especially in the more populated countries.

The Collapse of 2035 was a nasty business cycle that resulted in over twenty percent unemployment in the world's leading economies. What started as a minor recession escalated faster than economists thought possible. As usual in a recession, companies tried to get through it with a mix of layoffs and business process changes. At some point, the global reserve banks would stimulate the economy, money would be cheap, investment would follow, and everything would turn back to growth. That was the way it was supposed to work.

However, the human world was unprepared to react to a business cycle that was accelerated by AI and AI-enabled automation. As companies replaced more and more employees with technology in an attempt to retain profit growth, it became obvious that they didn't need those employees back ever again and, in fact, should probably cut more. Less and less people working made for fewer and fewer consumers, making those profits harder and harder to achieve, resulting in more and more layoffs.

As unemployment in the US jumped from five to ten percent in the first six months of 2035, the Fed dropped interest rates from four percent to one-point-five over the same period. The drop in interest rates did slow the decline in corporate profits and spurred some capital investments for more automation, but did nothing to stimulate hiring. By 2036, unemployment in the US was eighteen percent and climbing, interest rates were effectively zero, and economic panic was endemic across the globe.

The US Congress responded in 2036 with changes to the corporate tax structure that became known as the Murphy Act. The corporate tax rate was set on a progressive scale based on your profitability per full-time employee. If you had high profits but a low number of employees, you ended up handing over a bunch of those profits to the government. Those taxes were then earmarked for government-funded infrastructure programs that had their own employment requirements. In short, you could hire more employees than you needed or give the money to the government, and they would hire them for something else.

The scheme worked, and other major economies enacted their own variations of the model. Now in 2042, the average unemployment rate in the US hovered around two percent. If you wanted a job, you could get a job, although wage growth remained almost nonexistent. A highly profitable company like Artemis still paid plenty in taxes, but it would have been worse without the extra employees on the payroll. For some heavily populated countries, like India and Indonesia, the government-mandated push for employment was higher than elsewhere. Katherine's team there hated getting increased targets. They already had more people than they needed, and more people just meant more politics, more HR issues, more people asking for raises that would never happen.

The meeting ended, and Katherine was finally done for the day. Free, she grabbed her coat and headed to the elevator. She was meeting Harbrinder in Jack London Square. He had promised her dinner and an old-fashioned, two-dimensional movie. She stepped out the side door of Building 12 with a spring in her step and grabbed an AutoTram to the estuary water taxis.

The small electric water taxis were the best-kept secret in the Bay. They ran the mile or so between Artemis and Jack London Square. Four of them constantly buzzing back and forth. Tap your glass and get on board for a nine-minute ride. The little boats were completely automated and could carry a maximum of twenty people, but there were only a handful on board at the moment. She recognized a few people from campus, but the young woman in a bright pink broadcasting coil caught her eye. The estuary had its fair share of tourists, and this woman looked like one of them. Katherine couldn't help but smile at the coil. Some casters tried to hide it; the younger generation tended to show it off.

The Oakland Estuary divided Oakland and Alameda. It was about six miles long but averaged only a few hundred yards across. At its entrance, Katherine could see the huge hydrogen fuel-cell container ships unloading at the Port of Oakland. The mammoth ships were spewing out goods to waiting trucks and trains. Closer by, rowing clubs, sailboats, powerboats, and the occasional personal hydrofoil shared the water. The other end of the estuary used to simply end in mud flats and wetlands. Then in 1913, the Army Corp of Engineers dredged it out to officially make Alameda an island.

The estuary had historically attracted boaters with a blue-color feel. The fancy yachts tended to stay over in San Francisco, Sausalito, or Belvedere. Now all of that had changed. These days, land along the waterfront sold for tens of millions, and the estuary had become the playground for the wealthy. The Island side contained most of the wealth, but the gentrification had pushed deep into Oakland as well.

The town always seemed to miss the best of the previous Bay Area booms. Everything from the Gold Rush to Silicon Valley offered Oakland nothing more than leftovers. This time, however, Oakland was the gateway to the most valuable company in the world. For better or worse, there was a there there now.

The water taxi smoothly navigated the traffic and glided into Jack London Square with a chime. Automated side thrusters kept the vessel secured in its berth as Katherine stepped off and walked up the dock. Harbrinder's sailboat, *Blackfish*, was on the opposite end of the square, next to a famous bar, Heinold's First and Last Chance Saloon. Jack London himself used to frequent the saloon while working as a sailor and attending school. It was here that London met the cruel captain, Alexander McLean, who would inspire him to write the novel *The Sea Wolf*. Now, sea captains and authors had been replaced with the well-heeled pedestrians of the casting boom, rejoicing in restaurants, bars, and shops. She found herself smiling again as she walked past flirting pairs in the open air. She was about to be one of them. In a nice restaurant, not alone, not on business, enjoying the company of someone who just might be someone for her.

She'd been seeing Harbrinder for the last four months. It had been going well, which was nice. Katherine's last steady boyfriend was back in college, and even then she knew they wouldn't last past graduation. Since then it's been a series of mediocre affairs. When she was younger, she assumed it was obvious to men that work took top priority and they couldn't compete. She didn't worry about it. Any sort of intimacy was almost transactional. Both sides got what they wanted and moved on. Just over the last few years though, she felt like she might be missing out on something. She had far exceeded her own expectations professionally, so what was next? She wasn't really lonely, but wasn't she supposed to be able to share a deeper bond with someone? However now she was no longer young, unknown Katherine Tanaka. Now she was rich and powerful Katherine Tanaka, and it seemed to complicate getting truly close to anyone. So many men in her socio-economic class were looking for someone much younger than themselves or a stay-at-home personal assistant. She had absolutely no desire to become some old geezer's attendant. On the other hand, men with less money than Katherine—which was almost all men—seemed either intimidated or over-anxious to be with her. She admitted it might have been her reading too much into things, but she was never able to get to a place of relaxed companionship, much less a deep attachment.

Harbrinder was different though. He was fun to be around, only a few years older, seemed genuinely interested in her life, and had plenty of money of his own. She smiled to herself again and thought, *Well, maybe this is it?*

★★★

Harbrinder's glass chimed with two messages almost simultaneously. In his personal inbox was Katherine asking to be buzzed in through the dock gate. In his encrypted inbox was an unknown person simply saying, "Speed up your work." Bizarre. Not too many people could get that address. He mostly used it to communicate with third parties he funded anonymously. The few times he did use it, he was the one making requests. Strange, but for now he shut down the glass and turned his attention to Project Tanaka.

He had grown genuinely fond of Katherine. She was both attractive and intelligent, so it wasn't exactly a burden to spend time with her. Also, getting close to her wasn't some sort of elaborate scheme. He simply saw her at that Encinal Yacht Club charity event for the Singh Animal Shelters, knew who she was, and thought, *What the hell.* That was four months ago. Since then, it was clear that his instincts had paid off. He had gotten the occasional useful tidbit about the inner workings of Artemis for nothing more than the cost of a dinner. He rarely had to press. She knew he found her work "fascinating" and would freely offer an insight or two to keep the conversation going. Besides, God help him, literally fucking the system was amazing. It would all have to end badly, he knew, but until then? He might as well make the most of it.

"Ahoy! Permission to come aboard, Captain?"

Harbrinder rolled his eyes, collected himself, and popped his head out of the companionway.

"Always, beautiful. Just finishing some stuff up, and then I'll be right there. Can I get you a glass of wine or something?"

"No, I think I'm good for now," Katherine said as she slipped off her shoes and stepped onto the *Blackfish*.

"Hey, I made reservations for us at the Peruvian place on Webster if that works," Harbrinder shouted up, "but I'm open to whatever."

"Peruvian sounds good. I love their ceviche." Katherine took a seat in the cockpit and looked around the docks. It was just about evenly split between power and sailboats. At forty-two feet, the *Blackfish* was on the smaller side for this part of the marina. Across the way was the *Silas Clyde*, a forty-eight-foot fuel-cell power tug owned by another Artemis executive. It was styled as a working tug, but it was all luxury on the inside. The owner was notoriously single, and the *Clyde* had quite the reputation as a party boat.

"Any good gossip from the *Clyde*?"

"Oh, Katherine, you know it's against the law of the sea to share such information," Harbrinder said with a smile as he climbed out onto the deck and locked the companionway. "Let's just say that end of the dock gets a bit more foot traffic than the *Blackfish*."

They hopped back down onto the dock. Katherine took Harbrinder's arm as they walked to the gate. "It's funny," Katherine said, "growing up, the Bay was always right there, but I never thought too much about it. I mean, I never really went on the water. Just drove over the bridges and looked at it from time to time, I guess. Now I can't seem to get enough."

"Well, you do spend a lot of time on that island of yours. That would probably change your perception of the Bay."

"Yeah," Katherine laughed. "But even there, you might be surprised. A lot of people just come and go without a thought."

"No, I mean, I get it. When I was growing up and sailing with my dad, we were always blown away by how few people were on the water. If we snuck out on a weekday, we might see a dozen other boats on the water. A busy weekend might have a couple of hundred boats, which was still nothing for a body of water surrounded by eight million people. I guess everyone was just busy with their day-to-day lives."

"Yeah, I guess so. But more and more people like me seem to be noticing."

"True. And your island and the money on it is partially responsible for that. But there is still plenty of empty space out there beyond the estuary. Except maybe for where the damn ferries run."

Katherine smiled. "Oh, did you have another close encounter recently?"

"No comment."

They walked up to the restaurant and sat down outside. The last of the sun provided a small amount of warmth, about to be replaced by heat lamps. Harbrinder ordered a bottle of dry white wine to share as they looked through the menu, which featured local produce and seafood. California had, so far, been spared the worst impacts of climate change. The extremes were there, but on average, the state got just a little wetter and a little warmer. Parts of the Central Valley had to change up their crops, but agriculture had become even more profitable over the last two decades, partially due to crop failures elsewhere.

Southern California had the most dramatic change in the state as it became less dry and more sub-tropical. Summer storms, fed by rising sea temperatures, turned San Diego green in August. Warmer water had made its way up the coast past Santa Barbara to Point Conception, and there it stopped, blocked by the mass of California sticking its rear out into the sea and the cold Alaskan current that still flowed down that part of the coast. Compared to the dramatic changes in other parts of the world, California could count itself lucky.

They ordered the halibut ceviche with red onions, habaneros, and choclo.

"So how was your day?" Katherine asked.

"Pretty much the usual. I worked on my investments in the morning, took a fundraising call for the animal shelter, had lunch down here, and then took the *Blackfish* out for a spin. How about you?"

"Same, the usual. Ran, did a new hire presentation, a talent review, and spoke to the boss for a bit."

"Oh yeah, what did the boss want?"

"Not much. He's on his way to Uganda. Probably somewhere over Iowa right now, still on the first leg. He wanted to talk about the World Casting Association meeting coming up."

"Yeah, I heard about that. It was on my news feed."

"Yep, it's a big conference, and my team is pretty involved. Need to make sure it goes smoothly."

"Man, I don't know how you do it. I would hate to be caught up in all the politics of a big event like that. What do you think they can actually get done with all those different agendas?"

Katherine smiled. "Not much, to be honest. But we look for common ground where we can find it. If one or two real things come out of the meeting, that would be a win."

"The news report I read said there were a bunch of different committees and working groups," Harbrinder ventured. "What was one of them? Consumption, I think? Does that one decide what can be advertised or not or . . . ?"

"Yeah, that is part of what they do. It's around the standards of how influential advertising is allowed to be and to what audience."

"The other ones I heard about were a Safety and Security group, a Content group, and an Ethics group. But sounded like the Consumption group was the most powerful, don't you think?"

"Yeah, I mean, if you're really interested, the WCA has a public website that we maintain for them. All the working groups have their agendas up there. But I think the Ethics group is probably the most powerful."

"Really, why?"

Katherine seemed to catch herself and then continued.

"Well, we all want to make sure we're acting in the public's best interest, don't we?"

Harbrinder noted the stumble but didn't press. "Oh, you're no fun. I'm going to stick with Consumption as the most important."

"And I think you're silly for even caring. Even at Artemis, most people don't care that the meeting is even happening, much less what the committees are."

"Hey, if it's important to you, I'm interested. Besides, I don't get any exposure to the whole big company thing anymore. It's fascinating, I like talking to you about it, while, thankfully, I don't have to actually do any of it."

"Now you just sound spoiled."

"Oh, I am spoiled, but so are you. You don't have to do any of this anymore either, y'know. And I don't really understand why you do. Why not just cash out and come sailing with me?"

"I'll need a lot more wine before I can answer that question, Mr. Singh."

"Waiter!" Harbrinder smiled and ordered another bottle of wine.

After dinner, they took an AutoCab over to Grand Lake Theater to see a movie. Katherine loved this sort of thing. The movie was a remake of *True Grit*, an old-fashioned Western about a young girl seeking justice for her murdered father. While casting had both the money and the buzz, there was still room for this kind of entertainment. What casting didn't do well was any sort of fiction. At its core, casting was what they used to call Reality TV writ large. Even recordings of castings were not popular. It was technically possible to record a cast, but the playback felt synthetic. The human brain interpreted it as a manufactured experience. The closest media equivalent might be watching a poorly dubbed foreign film.

After the movie, the crowd filed out of the theater and started grabbing AutoCabs. Harbrinder and Katherine held hands as they queued up with the rest of the multitude.

"That was pretty good," Katherine said. "I still have to go with the 2010 version, but this was close. It was nice to get away for a couple of hours."

"Well, you could escape for a little longer if you'd like. My place is a lot closer than San Francisco."

"Hmmm," Katherine said. "That's tempting, but I'll take a rain check. It's Monday, and some of us have to actually work, y'know. Maybe this weekend?"

"I'll hold you to that, but let's say San Francisco? Wouldn't mind getting out of the East Bay for a bit."

"Maybe San Francisco then."

Their turn in the queue came up, and Harbrinder opened the door for Katherine. "You take this. I'm going to walk it."

"Thanks, and it was great seeing you." After a nice kiss, she hopped into the AutoCab and unrolled the window. As it pulled away, she teased, "Maybe this weekend."

Ah well, maybe this weekend, Harbrinder thought to himself as he began the ten-minute walk to his house near the Cleveland Cascade. He was really starting to like Katherine. Shame she had to work for the enemy. As he thought back on the evening, he thought it was interesting that she didn't see Consumption as the most powerful committee. After all, it was the group making people buy stuff, whether they wanted to or not. What could be more powerful than that? What did she say, Ethics? God, was she really that sweet? That naive? Did she really not see the damage casting was doing to people's free will?

Harbrinder strolled past the Heart & Dagger Saloon, paused, and decided a nightcap would be in order.

Jessie

Jessie saw Harbrinder walk through the door with a smug look on his face. It was crowded, and he could be a douche, but he was also a good tipper. She made eye contact with him while finishing another order.

"The Macallan and a Trumer," Harbrinder said with no further prompting.

Jessie poured the scotch neat and the beer into a frosted pint glass then placed them both in the service area and immediately started on her next order.

Harbrinder picked up the drinks and headed to the pool table. She kept the tab open. They both knew he would be back for at least one more round.

The Heart & Dagger had been on this corner in Oakland for a bit. Longer than Jessie had been alive anyway. Now thirty-one, she still remembered what it was like when she was younger. A bit rougher. More addicts like her.

The bar still carried a facade of its past, but it was harder to maintain the dive bar cred with a wealthier clientele and alcoholism now being more of a choice than a disease. Yet it still attracted people who liked their drink, and Harbrinder was certainly one of those people.

For her part, Jessie was grateful for the changes. Her life was better now. If that meant catering to the corporate casting clones from

Artemis, then so be it. Anyway, she owed her life to Artemis. These dipshits simply worked there.

Alcohol was the least of her problems, but it was the first one. She started drinking when she was fourteen. Her mom was too busy to notice or care. It was just the two of them, so she couldn't blame her for that. But for her stepfather? Yeah, her mom got some of the blame for him. He moved in when she was sixteen. That pervert sure noticed the drinking, and Jessie started turning to stronger ways to numb her mind. Eventually, she stopped going to school, and then she stopped coming home.

By the time she was twenty-two, she was working hard at dying young. A garbage pail addict. Up for whatever and doing what was needed to get there.

She was calling a lean-to on East 12th Street home when she noticed a team of clean-cut people distributing fliers around the encampment. The fliers promised a new treatment for anyone who wanted to quit. Free of charge. Open late. They gave an address a few blocks away.

Jessie laughed it off. Figured it was the Mormons or Jehovahs or something. Then one weekday night, her friend Jayla walked into their clinic and didn't come out.

It went on like that for a couple of weeks. Every few days, someone would go into that clinic and not come out. The only person she saw go in and come out again was Fisher. The old lunatic came running out, yelling about mind control and the government. People stopped going in for a while after that.

Jessie was nodding off in her lean-to on some blue fuf when she heard someone calling her name. It sounded like Jayla, but Jayla was gone.

"Go away!"

"Jessie! Jessie! Get out here and talk to me."

Jessie pulled back the tarp and stuck her head out. It really was Jayla, and she looked . . . clean. Physically clean, yes, but sober and healthier.

"Shit, Jayla, is that really you?"

"It's really me, and I have something I need to tell you about."

Jayla told Jessie about the clinic. How they scanned her head and then just "turned off" her addiction. She showed Jessie the fancy headband they gave her to use anytime the feelings came back. Jayla told her about the halfway house she went to that night. Now, they were paying Jayla to come out here and tell everyone else about it.

And then Jayla did tell everyone. Jessie watched as she went from tent to tent, person to person, spreading the same story.

Not that night, but soon after, Jessie was out of options and decided it was her turn to see what was inside the clinic.

Those people from Artemis treated her and the others well enough. As promised, her cravings went away immediately after the headband was fitted. However, some people had more to work out than substance addiction. Not everyone stayed in the program. Not everyone wanted to live. But most did.

Now, almost a decade later, the company's technology had made treating addiction a matter of simply putting on the right headset. Jessie no longer needed treatment. She didn't even like to drink anymore. Seemed childish to her now. Been there, done that. Like most people, her favorite Artemis product these days was the casting stuff.

"Hey, Jessie! Another round over here!" Jessie snapped out of her own mind and looked over at a douchey young Artemis employee in a large group. Those fucksticks had been there for hours without settling. But they would pay eventually. Everyone knew theft is bad.

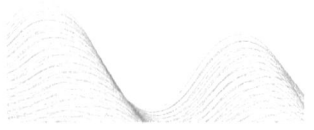

Henry

"Theft is bad" was the second embed. "Helping each other is good" was the first. Peter wrote those, but Henry maintained them now. At least for his domains, which were the two most important domains, the United States and Uganda. The United States was the first market and his home. Uganda was where everything was tested. Uganda was also very Christian, and Henry liked that. Henry knew that India was now the biggest market, but he thought his markets were still the most important, even though Bhavin was his friend.

Henry sat at the desk in his home office, staring at the computer glass, casually compiling an encrypted messaging framework while considering what to do. Henry was good at his job. Everyone said so, but he knew it was true. He wouldn't be working on Level 0 encryption and be in charge of the US and Uganda if he wasn't. He liked his work, which made things difficult right now. He felt he was helping people, and he made enough money to have a nice house for him and his mom. The work also aligned with his relationship with Jesus Christ, at least until recently.

Henry was different. Everyone said so, but he knew it was true. He knew his difference was part of what made him good at his job. Henry was very, very good at seeing patterns and doing math. He also knew it made it hard for him growing up. If it wasn't for his mother and Jesus, he knew he wouldn't be here today.

Peter hired him personally in 2030. They had met a few years earlier at UC Berkeley. Henry never went to college, but his mother took him to an Autism Society workshop. Mom was active in that community, and Henry liked some of the math problems at Berkeley. Henry showed Peter how good he was at picking out patterns from numbers, and Peter was impressed. When Peter called with a job, he wasn't surprised. His mom wasn't either.

His first job was in Level 1 encryption. He worked on quantum-resistant public-key cryptographic algorithms that secured individual medical coils. It would be very bad if someone could hack your coil. The AI was good at creating the algorithms, but Henry could spot patterns the AI missed. Maybe it was the way a human looked at it.

There was no Level 0 or Level 2 encryption at the time. Those came in 2034 when Artemis started casting. That was when they started needing embeds.

Henry never worked on Level 2 encryption. It was no sin of pride to say he was too good for Level 2. Level 2 encryption was for embedding advertising. It was important. You had to make sure the embeds worked but didn't work too much, only worked for a paying advertiser, and never worked on the wrong people or in the wrong geography. Making somebody crave something they were allergic to or could never, ever have was a sin. So it was important, but not as important as Level 1 or Level 0. Henry went from Level 1 straight to Level 0.

Level 0 was where the very best cryptographers worked with their own dedicated AI named Harpo. Harpo was a funny name. He didn't have much of a personality, but that was okay. Henry liked Harpo. Peter named him Harpocrates after the Greek god of secrets, but everyone just called him Harpo. Harpo could take datasets from any other Artemis AI, but he didn't share his with anybody, not even Caesar, the Sovereign AI.

Henry noticed an inverse relationship between the number of people and the importance of an encryption level. There were over a thousand people working in Level 2, over a hundred working in Level 1, and just eight here at Level 0. Henry didn't know who else knew about Level 0, but Peter said not to tell people it even existed, so he didn't think it was a lot. They just said they were working on part of the core operating system, which was true.

Harpo did a lot of the work, but Peter said it was important for people to make sure it was all going as it should. Each member of the team had different parts of the world they concentrated on. Each part of the world had different embeds. They made sure the embeds followed the rules set up by each government and OK'd by Peter. Harpo handled the execution. Mostly they made sure existing embeds ran smoothly, but every once in a while, they got to write a new embed with Harpo. That was usually the fun work, but the last one was not fun.

There weren't a lot of embeds. Peter said his deal with the government made it hard for anyone to do an embed. It had to be agreed upon by two different people, and those two people didn't agree a lot. Peter said this was on purpose. There were only six embeds for the United States:

- "Helping each other is good"

- "Theft is bad"

- "Racism is bad"

- "America is good"

- "Capitalism is good"

- "Work is good"

That was it. Not a lot, but the trick was to use them in the right way. It wasn't like the hacks in Level 2, where you could invoke a sudden artificial craving. Harpo kept it subtle but steady. He scanned for content where the embeds would naturally be more effective. He dialed it back in areas where it was too blatant. Henry kept an eye on all this and looked for patterns that might be obvious to people less talented than him.

Henry agreed with, or at least didn't mind, all of these embeds. If it was up to him, he would include the Ten Commandments. It was strange that they didn't at least include "Thou shalt not kill," but Peter said that might complicate things too much.

For Uganda, the standing list was even shorter. They did lots of testing there, but they had just two regular ones. Peter called it the First Two because it was the first two embeds ever. He said other countries used them a lot, so it was good to have them in the background for Uganda.

- "Helping each other is good"

- "Theft is bad"

It was one of the commandments (Thou shalt not steal) and the Golden Rule from the New Testament ("Do to others as you would have them do to you"). This was good. Henry liked this. Peter said there were some countries that didn't get any Level 0 embeds at all because they didn't ask for them. Henry thought this was strange and that everyone should get the First Two at least.

Then Peter said they needed to do a new embed for Uganda, and Henry did not like it.

- "Homosexuality is not a sin"

This was against what his mom and his pastor had always said. His pastor even showed him in the Bible that homosexuality was a sin. The Old Testament was really tough about it in Leviticus, saying people should be put to death. His pastor said that was before Jesus's love came to the world and in Romans it's just referred to as a sin. But it was a sin.

Henry told Peter he didn't want to do it, and they talked about it. Peter said homosexuality was illegal in Uganda, and people were going to jail just because of who they were. Peter said that wasn't fair and that he had made a deal with the Ugandan government. Artemis would hire more people in Uganda if they didn't make it illegal to be gay.

Henry didn't think people should go to jail for being gay and asked why the embed couldn't just say that. Peter said the Ugandan government could only change the law if Artemis convinced people that being gay wasn't a sin. Otherwise, the people would be mad at the government for making something legal that was a sin. He said they had to target the root of the issue.

Peter said that if Henry didn't want to write the embed with Harpo, he could ask Marcus to do it instead. That made Henry mad because he knew he was better at it than Marcus. Then Peter said he could take Henry off of Uganda, and that made Henry even madder.

Peter explained that sometimes you have to separate your personal beliefs from your work. Henry said that Peter didn't do that, which made Peter mad. Henry probably shouldn't have said that. Peter said he had to separate out personal and professional all the time and that it wasn't just him making all these decisions. Still, Henry felt that, at least this time, it was Peter making the decision.

Henry asked if Ibrahim had to do the same embed for Saudi Arabia. Being gay was also illegal there. Peter said no, they weren't doing it in Saudi Arabia. Henry asked why. Peter said it was because the Saudi government didn't agree with it. Henry wasn't sure if that was the only reason.

Henry ended up writing the embed with Harpo, but he let Harpo execute it without him really monitoring it. He didn't care if it worked or not, which felt bad.

Peter had been telling the Level 0 team that he was trying to make their jobs a little easier by standardizing the different embeds across countries. Right now it was very complicated and kept getting worse. More users, streaming more content within and between different countries. Harpo had to work really hard to make sure it worked right.

You didn't want someone in America getting a "Britain is good" embed every time they watched a British cast, even though they probably thought that already or they wouldn't be watching.

Peter said that was what the World Casting Association would be helping him do. Make the rules standard between countries. Henry thought this was a good idea at first, but then he wondered what those rules would be. What if "Homosexuality is not a sin" became a standard embed? What if it was "God is not real"? What if it was "Allah is the only God"?

He didn't think Peter would really make any of those standard embeds, but he started to see a pattern that he didn't like at all. He started to wonder if having only one system was a good thing after all. Henry liked order. He liked the idea of standardizing, but he didn't like the idea of those standards going against Jesus. It made him frustrated, and he could tell Peter knew it bothered him.

Henry wouldn't want to ever betray Peter. Peter was nice to him. But even Peter wasn't as important as Jesus. So Henry started to wonder if there should be a new network. Maybe even a JesusNet that really did embed the Ten Commandments and the love of Jesus into everything? That sounded like heaven on earth and good work for someone like Henry. He could handle both the Level 0 embeds and the Level 1 security. There wouldn't need to be any Level 2 work because there wouldn't ever be any advertising on JesusNet. He then realized it wouldn't be betraying Peter because they wouldn't be taking away any advertising money.

Henry didn't know how to start a new network, but he did know about the OpenCast Project. He knew they never did advertising. Maybe if their user base got a little bigger and their software got a little better, Henry could make JesusNet from the OpenCast Project?

So he spent his free time at home, praying about what to do and researching the OpenCast Project. He built a custom coil and rolled his own version of the open-source code. He saw there were plenty of good people doing normal things on the OpenNet. People who just didn't want advertising and couldn't afford the subscription cost. Other people were there because they believed in conspiracies about government control on the SmallNet and BigNet. Some of these people had silly ideas about what the government was doing. Some other people had the right ideas, but more people believed the silly ideas. He also saw some very bad things on the OpenNet. People casting while hurting other people. People casting while being hurt. People doing very bad sexual things. Henry would need to work on getting these bad people to become good people thanks to the love of Jesus.

As Henry looked deeper into OpenCast, he saw a pattern. He liked looking for patterns, and this one had the name Harbrinder Singh on it deep within several projects. People seemed to think he was important.

"Dinner, Henry," his mom said from the kitchen.

"Coming."

Henry thought he should tell this Harbrinder to work harder, but he didn't want to be caught doing that in case Peter found out. For Henry, it was easy to take a standard encrypted messaging account and then put his own additional layer of encryption behind it to make it virtually impossible for anyone to ever tie it back to him. On the other hand, finding Harbrinder's commercially encrypted account was easy for someone like Henry.

He opened up the command line on his freshly compiled, double-encrypted messaging framework. He typed in "Speed up your work" and then went to have dinner with his mom.

Kelly

K elly cleared the table and asked Henry if he needed anything else.
"No, thank you. I'm just going to go work on some things."

"That sounds fine, Henry. I'll do the dishes, and then I plan on catching that cast later on tonight."

"Okay, Mom. Love you."

"Love you too, sweetheart."

Kelly headed to the kitchen to get the dishes done. Henry went back to the converted bedroom that he used as his home office. He probably had enough computer equipment back there to power a small data center, and certainly enough to power his own personal AI, but Kelly didn't mind. It was his money, and Henry was a good boy.

Henry bought this nice house on the Island in 2036, just for the two of them. It was a crazy amount of money to spend. She thought they would have been better off buying somewhere cheaper, but Henry wanted to be close to work. She couldn't fault him. It'd been a good investment, so far at least.

As she worked alone in the large kitchen, Kelly tried to remember she had nothing to complain about. Her life was good. It's just that she didn't fit in with many other people on the Island. She was fifty-eight, divorced, went to church, lived with her adult son, and didn't work. She just took care of Henry, who needed a lot of taking care of for a genius. He might be able to do a logic puzzle faster than anyone, but he didn't know, or maybe didn't care to know, pragmatic things like how to pay the bills or shop for groceries. So Kelly took care of all that as she always had, but now with Henry's money.

Growing up in Livermore in the 90s, Kelly had enjoyed life. Enjoyed it a little too much, she supposed. She loved going to concerts, having a few beers, and messing around with her boyfriend, Brian. She was smart enough to go to a four-year college straight out of high school, maybe even on a scholarship, but didn't particularly want to. Life was good, and she didn't see a need to change things. Working at Target, living with her parents, and taking a couple of classes at Las Positas Community College was the sum of her ambition at twenty-one.

God help her, sometimes she longed for those days. She found herself reliving them more and more through casting. The one she was going to attend tonight was a concert on the BigNet. Frazzle was a band popular with people half her age. She would be attending through a fan caster going with all her girlfriends. The BigNet would always pick out someone who was profiled to be genuinely excited to go and give them a once-in-a-lifetime VIP experience as long as they agreed to cast the whole time. She couldn't wait to feel the excitement, all ad-free, thanks to Henry. She sighed as she remembered being that girl, minus the VIP treatment, of course.

But she stopped being that girl after she messed up. No, she shouldn't think of it that way. Let's just say God had different plans for her when Brian got her pregnant.

Brian was a good time, but Henry's brains didn't come from that side of the family. At least he tried to do the right thing to begin with. In retrospect, Kelly knew marrying Brian was a bad idea, but what else was she supposed to do? Her parent's religion had rubbed off on her enough that she wouldn't even think about getting an abortion. Giving the baby up for adoption didn't seem right either, especially after her mom told her she couldn't stand never seeing her own grandchild.

So they got married, Brian started working full-time at the tire shop, and with a little help from her parents, they got a one-bedroom apartment in downtown Livermore for themselves. Kelly kept working right up to a week before her due date, and then Henry was born. They named Henry after Kelly's grandfather, but Brian told everyone it was after Hank Hill from the *King of the Hill* cartoon. Brian was the only one who thought that was funny.

Things were good for the first year or so. Henry was a good, if quiet, baby. They could take him with them anywhere, and he never caused a fuss. He would just sit in his car seat, playing with his baby shapes. Kelly's mom would watch him when Kelly had to work or when she wanted to go out with Brian.

It was Kelly's mom who first noticed that Henry might be different. Henry didn't seem to want to engage with people or try to talk, he just wanted his baby shapes. Kelly saw these things too, but she didn't even think about it being normal or not. It was just what Henry did, and he was the only baby she had ever been around. He seemed happy, so that was enough for her.

Her mom was with her at Henry's eighteen-month checkup and talked to the doctor about Henry's behavior. The only sounds Henry made were crying when something was wrong, and even that was rare. He didn't want to look directly at anyone except his mom and grandma. To Kelly's unease, the doctor said there could be an issue, but it was too early to tell. He recommended letting Henry engage with more children and see how he developed.

It was after this that the real differences between Kelly and Brian started to emerge. Kelly told Brian that there might be an issue, and his reaction was all about Brian. He kept going on that he didn't want to have a retard for a son and that this was just so embarrassing. Kelly was embarrassed too, but she was embarrassed by Brian, not Henry.

She did what the doctor recommended and started bringing Henry to playgroups. She would place him on a mat, and he would immediately demand his baby shapes. His only reaction to other children was if they tried to play with his baby shapes too. That would make Henry cry.

Kelly stopped going to the playgroups and started reading more about autism. She recognized some of the signs in Henry but also learned that everyone "on the spectrum" was different. She started engaging in online forums with other parents in similar situations. She found a kinship there even as she grew more certain that Henry would have a hard road in front of him.

Brian would work all day, walk to the apartment for dinner, and then she wouldn't see him again until he came home drunk, trying to crawl into bed with her. He rarely engaged with Henry anymore, even on the weekends. She tried to keep it together, to have someone else on her team, but Brian's behavior disgusted her more and more. He must have felt her distaste for him grow, and that made her feel guilty sometimes. Honestly, though, Brian was always looking for an excuse to walk away. Probably easier on his fragile ego to blame her for Henry's problems, blame her for the lack of affection, blame her for trapping him.

One Friday night when Henry was three, Brian just didn't come home. God forgive her, but she was glad. He came by the next day and got his stuff. He said he was moving out and wanted a divorce. She just stared at him and held Henry. No shouting, no crying.

She gave notice on the apartment the next day. A few weeks later, she was living back at her parents with Henry. She heard Brian was out in Tracy with some woman he met at the bar.

As Henry grew, Kelly started finding her rhythm again. Despite his father disappearing, Henry had a lot of support. Kelly's parents welcomed them into their home, and the local schools had a good autism program. Perhaps most importantly, Kelly started going back to her parent's church again for the first time since high school. There she found an accepting community for both her and Henry. A community that she easily dismissed when she was younger and didn't have a care in the world. People at the church acknowledged their shared struggles while supporting each other through the love of Christ. Henry would always go with Kelly and sit and listen quietly to the sermons. He seemed to like the order of everything, the way the services always followed a similar pattern, and the rules that the Bible passed down. Henry began to open up, if only slightly, to the world around him.

By the time Henry was a teenager, his "superpower" with numbers and patterns had become clear. It was also clear that he couldn't stay in public school any longer. He was sheltered from most of the bullying in his Special Day Class, but he still didn't engage with other kids. He was never aggressive or mean, but he was frustrated and angry almost every day. He would just come home and tell her school was so stupid, which was a normal enough teenage thing to say, but Kelly knew Henry meant something else. He meant the math parts were too easy and the rest of it was just not necessary at all in Henry's mind.

Kelly felt it was her responsibility to help Henry be the best version of himself he could be. She stopped working again to home-school Henry in a math and computer science-focused curriculum. The schoolwork went quickly over her head, but she found good resources online to keep Henry engaged. By the time Henry was sixteen, he was taking free online math classes from MIT while earning certificates in Python and SQL. Still, she had a hard time keeping him focused on anything he wasn't interested in. For example, he stopped working on a Java certificate halfway through because he had "figured it out already." Henry was so smart, but she still worried about his future. It was hard to picture him holding a job if he stopped everything halfway through and didn't want to interact with his coworkers.

She managed to get him a home school high school diploma when he was eighteen, but then had to figure out what to do next. She tried to keep Henry engaged with various online classes and encouraged him to write his own software while she increased her involvement with the Bay Area Autism Society. She felt that the tech-focused Bay Area, of all places, must have a use for someone like Henry.

In 2027, when Henry was twenty-one, they went to a "Math and Autism" workshop at UC Berkeley. There would be other people on the spectrum Henry's age, and Kelly thought there might be some advanced math materials he could pick up.

In between sessions, they went and sat in the lobby. Henry had his laptop with him and was playing the "Pi Game" as he called it when Peter Graham caught Kelly's eye. Peter walked over and introduced himself. He said he was a professor in the computer science department but was also fascinated by autism. Kelly asked him if he had a child or a loved one with autism as well, and Peter responded no, that it was the way autism worked in the brain that fascinated him. He said it was related to the piriform cortex, an incredibly complex area of the brain that also happened to relate to the sense of smell.

Kelly didn't know what to make of that.

"Well, this is Henry, and he can smell just fine."

"I'm sure he can. Hello, Henry!"

"Hello," Henry responded without looking up from his laptop.

"What are you doing there?"

"Pi game."

"Oh, that's just something he does to keep busy," Kelly said.

"He looks at twelve-digit numbers flashing up on a laptop?" Peter asked.

"It's a little more than that. Henry, why don't you do it out loud, sweetheart?"

"Okay," Henry said, and then, "299 . . . 8491 . . . 2852 . . ."

"That doesn't match any of the number patterns on the screen. What are you doing?"

"It's where they belong," Henry said. "It's their place . . . 1424."

"You see," Kelly said. "Henry wrote a program that flashes random twelve-digit sequences from the first ten thousand digits of Pi. Then Henry guesses what position the first digit in that sequence would be in Pi. So that last number string started with the 1424 digit of Pi."

"What, that's amazing. How accurate is he?" Peter asked.

"I think I've missed five," Henry interjected.

"Just five times today?" Peter asked.

"Just five times ever," Henry said.

Kelly smiled at the look on Peter's face and explained a little bit of Henry's background. How smart he was, but also how he had a hard time keeping focused on any problem if it was too easy. Peter said he was working on something really complicated that might be of interest to Henry someday. He asked for her contact info. Maybe it was just a pickup line, but Kelly figured it couldn't hurt.

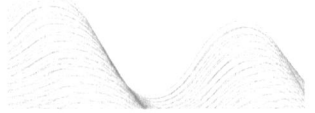

Peter

*M*aybe I should have Henry killed? Peter thought to himself and immediately grimaced. What the hell had he become? *My God, thinking about killing someone.*

The really disturbing thing was Peter knew how easy it would be. He could just mention a potential breach and Henry's name to his government liaison. The problem would just go away. Nothing more would need to be said, but an AutoCab would malfunction and drive into the water. Or something heavy would fall off the back of a truck. Maybe an electrical fire at night in his house. Even if someone thought his death was suspicious, it would never, ever get back to Peter. He had a license to kill, and he hated it.

He knew he fucked up with that Uganda embed. He was just trying to do the right thing, but that always seemed to backfire. Hell, he thought he was doing the right thing creating casting. He thought he was doing the right thing hiring Henry. He was mad at himself because he should have known Henry would object, but Peter was the boss, damn it, and shouldn't it be that easy? He couldn't even fire Henry. Firing someone from Level 0 would just be the same as having him killed once the Feds found out. He couldn't even piss him off and pull him off of his domains because an upset Henry with Level 0 access would be dangerous to everyone. And he could already tell Henry was distracted. If Henry screwed up casting in Uganda, that could be bad. If he screwed up the United States, that could be world-changing. He had

Harpo monitoring for any anomalies, but he wasn't sure how to get out of this one. Maybe once the embed ran for a year and homosexuality was decriminalized in Uganda, he could turn it off and make Henry happy again? God, he couldn't believe the lives of millions of people were revolving around the happiness of a thirty-six-year-old autistic man. Or, for that matter, a sixty-year-old ex-Berkeley professor.

Peter's life had stopped being his own in 2033 when he filed the patent for casting. He and Linda had just turned the medical industry upside down with the use of rTMS. The blind could see, the deaf could hear, and billions of dollars in pharmaceuticals had become obsolete. Artemis was a household name. So naturally his casting patent application was immediately under the microscope. Analysts were tripping over themselves to determine exactly what "the use of repetitive transcranial magnetic stimulation to reliably broadcast brain functionality over IP networks" really meant. Was it telepathy? Could you control another human being remotely? Was Peter sending the human mind into an AI?

So it wasn't too much of a surprise when his first, week-long, official meeting with the US Government had forty people on the US side. Representing Artemis, it was just Peter, Frank Kovacs, and Dominic Pappas, Artemis's chief legal counsel. Dominic had only engaged the Food and Drug Administration and the Federal Communications Commission, but the room was full of people who were vague about titles. It took most of the first day just to make sure everyone was truly authorized to be there and under a Non-Disclosure Agreement.

By the end of the second day, Peter had outlined what casting did and what the business model looked like. The hardware would be $1499 for an audience coil and $2999 for a broadcast coil. The monthly subscription would be $199. For that, users would have unlimited access to both user-generated (the SmallNet) and premium (the BigNet) content.

The next three days were an exhausting series of deep dives on the technology.

Feds: Could you hack someone's thoughts?

Artemis: No.

Feds: What parts of the brain does casting impact?

Artemis: Those related to sight, sound, touch, and feelings through the release of hormones. Not smell, unfortunately. The piriform cortex has been tough to decode.

Feds: Could you hack a stream?

Artemis: Effectively no, but theoretically possible.

Feds: Could you record a cast?

Artemis: Yes, but it sucks.

Feds: Could someone die if they get a hormone spike their body can't handle?

Artemis: Brain scans and health records allow for personalized fail-safes for each user.

Feds: Could you artificially make someone feel something that wasn't in the stream?

Artemis: Yes, but the stream is encrypted to prevent that.

Feds: But you could do it on your end if you wanted to?

Artemis: Yes, but we have no desire to do that, and it often comes across as artificial to the end-user anyway.

Feds: No desire? How do we know you won't be artificially injecting whatever you want into the stream?

Artemis: We are open to government monitoring.

Feds: Can we have a couple of our people try it out so we know what we're dealing with?

Artemis: Yes, we can do a brain scan and fitting next week.

The government people left and said they would schedule another meeting in two weeks after they had a chance to try the technology. It was in that next meeting that everything started to fall apart.

On the appointed day, Peter, Frank, and Dom headed back to the Federal Building in Oakland. Peter walked into the same large conference room, prepared for another grilling. Inside sat just three people on the government side. None of them were from the FDA or the FCC. One of them had tried out casting the previous week. One of them wasn't even in the initial meetings. Now Peter was getting creeped out.

Dominic started the meeting by asking for the new guy to introduce himself and sign an NDA before they continued. The new guy just smiled, introduced himself as George, and signed the NDA with G. Washington. Dominic stared down at the paper with a frown, but before he could say anything, George said, "Look, we just have some questions."

Peter put a hand on Dominic and said, "Okay, we figured there would be some additional questions. Go ahead."

"All right, when are you all going to start advertising to your user base?"

Frank perked up; this was what he wanted all along.

"Never," Peter replied. "This is a subscription-only model."

"Bullshit. At some point, you will start advertising. Maybe you'll miss a revenue target. Or maybe you'll want to grow faster than a subscription model allows, but at some point, you will start advertising."

"I disagree. We are a highly profitable company. We have plenty of revenue on the medical side. We can do this at cost or even at a loss for a long time."

"I don't believe you," George said. "You told us you could artificially inject enhanced feelings for something if you wanted to. At some point, you will do it. At best, it will be for advertising, at worst it will be whatever personal agenda you have."

"No, we won't, and as I said, we are open to government monitoring."

"And I think you're lying to us. I think we should not only deny you a broadcasting permit, but I think your patent itself should be considered a matter of national security. As such, under USC section 1498, we should exercise eminent domain and impound all of your lab work."

With that, George and the two other men got up and left the room. Peter, Frank, and Dominic were all left staring at each other with shocked looks.

"Well, that went well, don't you think?" Peter said.

Dominic spent the next week frantically pinging his government contacts trying to get another meeting while simultaneously looking into how to sue the Federal Government in case this thing went sideways.

Peter and Frank tried to figure out what the hell just happened.

"As a sales guy, I think this was just their opening bid in negotiations. Playing tough, to begin with," Frank said eventually.

"But negotiating for what? We said we're open to government monitoring. What more do they want?" Peter replied.

"I don't know," Frank said. "Maybe we'll find out in the next meeting."

And then it started to click in Peter's head. They wanted more than monitoring. They wanted control.

Peter remembered walking the two miles home from the Artemis HQ that night to the tiny house he and Linda rented off of Main Street in Alameda. They had lived there since 2029 after selling the brown shingle in Berkeley. It broke their hearts to sell that house, but they wanted to put all their money into the company and be as close as possible to work. Now, four years and a good deal of financial success later, they just hadn't found the time to move again. Linda took the lead in the ever-expanding medical side of the business while Peter concentrated on casting. It seemed that all they ever did was work, so where they slept was not a priority. Still, Peter enjoyed taking the time to walk home when he could. Tonight, he needed the fresh air to clear his head.

As usual, Linda got home late, and they discussed their day as Peter reheated some food for her.

"I think we're ready to go into Device Review with the FDA for the anti-addiction coil," Linda said as she scarfed down some pasta. "Between that and the pain relief coil, I think fentanyl's days are finally numbered."

"Wow, that's amazing! Congratulations and cheers to that!" Peter said as he raised a glass of red wine.

"Yep, cheers indeed," she said as she raised her own glass. "I'm going to ask Katherine to reach out to the Homeless Action Center in Oakland. I want to get coils into the right hands as soon as they're approved. So how about you? Did you hear anything back from the Feds?"

"No, not yet, but I think we will soon. And I think I know what they want and what I have to do."

Peter laid out his thoughts on how everything would go down as Linda gradually stopped eating and stared at him. By the time he was done, Linda was silently looking down at the floor.

"You could be wrong, you know," Linda said.

"Yeah, I could be."

"I knew we shouldn't have messed with casting. We should have stuck with medical."

"You're probably right," Peter admitted.

"Yeah, I probably am. Look, I love you, but I don't want anything to do with casting. I'm helping people in a very direct, very real way on the medical side. All this casting is a huge potential distraction, and I don't want anything to do with it."

"I understand. I won't involve you any more than absolutely necessary, but I don't see any other way out."

"You could be wrong, you know."

"I could be, but I don't think I am."

The Feds finally agreed to another meeting about a week later. Peter let Dom and Frank know how he thought this would play out and that he would take the lead in negotiations.

They were done with the large conference room this time and were directed to a private consulting room within the Federal Building. George Washington was waiting there with his two sidekicks.

"Hello again, Mr. Graham," George said. "Are you here to tell us why we shouldn't pull your patent?"

"You're not going to pull the patent," Peter said. "And you are going to approve our broadcasting license; you just want something in return."

"Oh really now," George laughed. "Are you saying this is all about a bribe?"

"No, I wish it were that simple. You want something more than that; you want control."

George kept smiling. "If we wanted control, we could just take it. Isn't that where this is heading, Mr. Graham? We're getting ready to take control of your labs."

Peter sighed. "No, you are not. Can we please stop fucking around? Let me tell you what is going to happen."

Peter sat up, leaned forward with his elbows on the table, and continued. "First of all, you are not going to claim eminent domain over the patent. You can't afford to take that risk. Between my patent application and the rTMS products already on the market, I can one hundred percent guarantee that engineers both inside and, critically for you guys, outside of this country are already reverse engineering my work.

"If you try to seize anything, Dom here will sue, you'll lose access to our expertise, and everything just stops and sits, maybe for years. Meanwhile, in China and the rest of the world, they will be recreating what I did, and you will have multiple rabbits, none of which are American, to get back in the hat. And, gentlemen, I guarantee these rabbits will multiply like crazy."

George just stared at Peter.

"Now, what you really want to do is approve our broadcast license, but you want some level of control over what is broadcast. So you threaten us with this eminent domain crap until at some point you figure we'll be grateful if you just let us keep our own technology. So grateful, that we are willing to follow whatever rules you lay out to start broadcasting. Well, now that we all agree the eminent domain threat isn't real, where does that leave us? I guess you could delay the broadcast license, but that really just does the same thing, doesn't it? If we can't broadcast, someone, somewhere outside the United States eventually will. America will lose the first-mover advantage because of your bullshit. Tick tock, guys, time is ticking until the window closes on having a centralized, US-based network."

George kept staring at Peter. Peter gave it a full thirty seconds of silence before continuing.

"Now, I can guess what rules you guys want to put in place. You showed a lot of 'concern' over artificially injecting emotional reactions to certain subjects. Do you want me to go first on the rules, or would you like to knock off the crap and just tell us?"

George stared. Peter said nothing.

"You need to do advertising," George finally said, "and we need some level of control over how effective it is and what is advertised. We're fine with an ad-free premium tier, but need a majority of the user base receiving ads."

"Yeah, I figured on that, gotta keep the wheels of capitalism rolling in a post-scarcity economy," Peter said.

"It's a little more than that. Give us some credit, Mr. Graham. Believe it or not, we are the good guys."

"Oh really?"

"Yeah, look, we are not quite as 'post-scarcity' as Berkeley-boy here might think. The coming decades will see a lot of changes in what foodstuffs and luxury items are available. And which ones are sustainable to consume. You like that word, don't you, Mr. Graham? Sustainable? Well, we happen to see your technology as a way to nudge people toward a more sustainable mode of consumption. Also, I'm sure you truly believe you will never advertise. The history of every other main-stream social network that has ever existed might suggest otherwise. We would prefer to get ahead of it from the start."

It was Peter's turn to stare for a moment. "What else?"

"We might need you to interject some concepts for the good of society. Again, we see some rough water ahead. Between climate change and the job market being nuked by AI, we're going to need all the help we can get convincing people not to lose their shit. Society is changing rapidly, Mr. Graham, and there is nothing new about using communication for change management."

"Concepts for the good of society? What concepts, and who gets to decide that they're good?" Peter said.

"We don't know the exact concepts yet. We'll let you know what we want to do, and you can make it happen."

"No," Peter said.

"No?"

"No, I'm not going to just be an order taker. There might be things that you guys want, like 'vote democratic' or 'vote republican,' that I'm not going to just inject into the streams. Also, 'George Washington,' I don't even know who the hell you really are. I'm not going to do anything unless I know this is sanctioned at the highest levels of government. Then there are the practical considerations. The embeds would have to be simple and subtle unless you want people to be able to tell they're artificial."

"Then what would you suggest?" George replied.

"I don't know, but we need some say on this side as well."

Peter, Frank, and Dom spent the next week working with the government trio to create the structure that was largely in use today. For advertising, Artemis would receive guidelines on what products could be advertised and on how pervasive that advertising could be. These guidelines would be maintained by the FCC and be available for public scrutiny. Privately, Artemis agreed to set monthly subscription pricing to ensure at least fifty percent of the user base received advertising.

The "good of society" embeds, which would become known as Level 0, would remain confidential. Beyond those in the room, Peter said he would need to bring in at least four engineers to start and a dedicated, powerful AI to execute. He said Linda, as his majority co-shareholder, as well as some members of Artemis's senior staff, would need to be informed.

The most contentious part of the entire project was deciding who got to pick the Level 0 embeds. George wanted to simply hand Peter a list. Peter refused on the basis of "Who the hell is George?" Peter wanted the ability to veto any embeds and suggest his own. George refused on the basis of "Who the hell is Peter?"

Both Peter and George agreed the rabbit was out of the hat and they had to move forward with something. Peter couldn't kill the whole concept at this point even if he wanted to. He was resigned to damage control. George knew he needed Artemis's expertise and an American company to be in the first mover position. Neither of them were happy about it, but they ended up with an outline that was ultimately adopted.

Peter insisted on elected officials being involved while somehow maintaining confidentiality. The Senate majority and minority leaders were selected as both regularly dealt with confidential national security issues. He hoped having both involved would stem extremism from either side.

Peter didn't get his veto or the ability to directly suggest embeds, but he did get some key concessions. Both senators had to agree on the embed, and no more than one embed could be added or changed every six months. There was also a hard limit of ten total embeds in the system at any one time. Peter said these limits were based on what the AI could handle. That was possibly true, but in the years to come, he would make sure the system was architected with these limits in place. There were also practical issues on the complexity of the embed and best practices in implementation that Peter would refine over time.

To ensure compliance, the government would receive the decrypt keys to Level 0 and Level 2 embeds so they could see what was inside any given stream.

By 2034, Artemis got the go-ahead, and Peter turned his life fully over to the politics of casting.

The first embed request was surprisingly benevolent. Seemed almost socialist to Peter, but he had a feeling the two Senators were just testing the waters of an unknown system. It was simply "Helping each other is good." Peter wrote the embed himself with the help of a new dedicated AI, Harpocrates. It ran for six months and all seemed well. Then Peter got the next embed "Theft is bad". This was more along the lines of what he had expected.

In all the years since, he had only received four additional Level 0 embed requests in the United States. They were all a reaction to current events. In order, they were:

- "Racism is bad." Another pleasant surprise, but racial tensions were starting to boil over as the economy soured at the start of the Collapse of 2035. When you weren't blaming AI, you blamed people who looked different than you.

- "America is good." Peter was waiting for this one, and by the middle of 2035, the politicians felt people needed a reminder.

- "Capitalism is good." Another one that Peter figured would show up eventually. Eighteen percent unemployment and all the money going to those who controlled the AIs would cause people to forget this.

Then there was a pause in requests as things in the country seemed to stabilize. He expected some sort of change after the Second Korean War, but nothing came. Then, in 2040, he received the latest request.

- "Work is good." Maybe this was due to record-low unemployment. He didn't ask, but Peter had a sinking feeling that it was mostly related to the castaways. These were people who spent their lives jumping from cast to cast, addicted to the emotions of others, never contributing their own lives to society.

Overall, just seven embeds in eight years. Much less than he was afraid of in 2033. Perhaps the two senators had a hard time agreeing, which was exactly what he was hoping for.

For the global roll-out, Peter, Frank, and Dom divided up the world and hit the road throughout 2034. The discussions with America's closest allies were surprisingly straightforward. He sensed George, or somebody like him, was working behind the scenes. Each government simply wanted a variation of the deal the US had already made. By 2035, the EU, the UK, Canada, Japan, Australia, and New Zealand were all actively casting.

For countries that were less aligned with the United States, they had to start from scratch. The more hostile countries just banned casting outright (China/Iran) or had a soft band (Russia) that prohibited the sale of coils in the country but allowed the wealthy to purchase and use coils from elsewhere. China famously developed its own closed system that rolled out in 2037, lending credence to Peter's assumption that copying his patent started almost immediately. Russia also had its own system by 2039, but adoption was sparse, even within Russia.

A few countries let Artemis cast without any concessions outside of some pretty standard advertising guidelines. Most countries, however, sensed a deeper opportunity and wanted to talk.

India was the toughest by far. It was Artemis's largest potential market, and Peter knew full well they could replicate Artemis's capabilities over time. However, by 2037 they had a deal similar to the United States that gave India control over both the types of advertising and a set number of Level 0 embeds selected by committee. Artemis also had to build a development center with a minimum of five-thousand full-time employees and ensure both Level 0 and Level 2 embeds were tailored for different regions of the country.

Elsewhere, the negotiations usually followed a similar script, but they had much less pressure to comply. In some cases, Peter got his veto on embeds. In other cases, he had to deal with a one-party system. In a few cases, he simply didn't operate in a country because it wasn't worth it.

That was initially the case in Costa Rica. The president at the time wanted some pretty direct and authoritarian embeds to solidify his rule. Peter refused and walked away from negotiations.

A month later, the president of Costa Rica held a news conference explaining that America was using Artemis to control the world by putting thoughts into people's minds.

Katherine had her hands full for a while with that one, but she did a good job of deflection. She portrayed El Presidente as someone who didn't understand the technology and was confusing Artemis's well-documented advertising with something deeper. It would give the conspiracy hacks fodder for years to come, but nothing more came from it. Meanwhile, the Costa Rican elite, dependent on US trade, made sure Costa Rica had a new president after the next election.

All of these deals around the world made casting both the most powerful and the most complicated communication platform ever seen. Combined with the medical innovations, it also made Peter and Linda the wealthiest people in the world and Peter arguably the most powerful.

Yet he was exhausted and sick of it. The whole Uganda thing was just another example of the dance he'd been doing for the last eight years. Make a wrong decision and people's lives were ruined. He never wanted this kind of pressure; he just wanted to bring the world closer together. He kept trying to do the right thing, but what that was wasn't always clear.

Along with Linda, he dropped the CEO title in 2039 to let Frank take over. The public statement was they wanted to spend more time working on pure research and philanthropy. In Linda's case, this was true. In Peter's case, it was to work full-time on getting himself out of the middle of casting without ruining the world. The World Casting Association was his ticket out. If he could get it set up properly, it might even achieve his original goal of using casting to bring people closer together. At the very least, it would take decisions like Uganda out of his hands and Henry's whims.

He decided to take the multi-rotor over to Artemis in the morning and see how Katherine was doing with the Ethics Committee at the WCA.

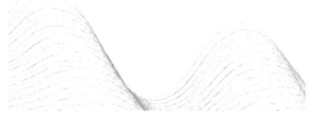

Harbrinder

"Still stuck at fifteen percent?" Harbrinder said.

"Yes, here in Korea, that is true," Jun said, "however, have you seen the latest numbers from Vietnam and Malaysia? OpenCast has grown to seven and five percent of total casting in those countries."

Jun was the Chairman of the Association for Mental Freedom, based in Korea. Harbrinder had been supporting the AMF, both technically and financially, since its founding shortly after the war. The charter of the AMF was to ban casting embeds, including ads, and standardize casting technology globally. In practice, that meant the AMF was a marketing arm for OpenCast.

"Yeah, that's good, Jun, but growth stalling in Korea still concerns me. If we are hitting a ceiling there, we'll likely hit similar limits elsewhere."

Harbrinder didn't understand how Artemis remained the most popular platform in Korea of all places. The war was a clear example of the dangers of casting and, in particular, what could happen when a small group controlled what was cast. If millions of people dying wouldn't wake people up, what would?

"We don't know that, my friend. Growth elsewhere could unlock Korea. The virtuous cycle will begin. We are making progress," Jun said.

Harbrinder decided to let it go. "What else do you have for me, Jun?"

"We'd like to see more hardware dev-kits in Thailand. We think if you could make them available at, or possibly even below cost, it could lead to significant growth in that country."

Harbrinder did some quick math in his head. "Yeah, we can do that. At cost anyway. Maybe below, but I can't promise it."

Harbrinder wrapped up the call and then went back to thinking about the OpenCast market share in Korea.

The seed for the Second Korean War was planted in 2038 when a clone of the Chinese People's Network made its way into North Korea. After the death of her brother, Kim Yo-jong took over the leadership of the country. She embraced the use of casting to "demonstrate the power of single mind unity to complete the socialist revolution" and to "align the people against the barbarians of Japan, America, and their South Korean puppets." Low-cost coils were manufactured and distributed to around eight percent of the population by the first month of 2039.

The North Korean state failed to realize just how powerful casting could be until it was too late. Leadership saw it simply as another propaganda tool that should be used to maximum effect. Unfortunately, someone in power decided to turn up the volume with a particularly strong series of anti-Western casts in mid-February. By February 17th, 2039, large numbers of North Koreans had spontaneously gathered near the DMZ. State Security forces swarmed in to disperse the group, but they were horribly outnumbered. The regular North Korean Army seemed to be divided between those supporting the mob and those trying to control them. Finally on February 20th, over two-hun-dred-thousand North Koreans, many of them civilians armed only with clubs, stormed over the border. Despite the lack of coordination, the numbers themselves would have been overwhelming in most situations. However, against a professional South Korean force, in the most heavily fortified part of the world, it was a blood bath. Crazed men and women running across minefields toward set defenses with AI-enabled fire control had no chance. Tens of thousands of North Koreans, blinded by a casting-fueled rage, died in the first hour. South Korea and its American allies launched massive non-nuclear counterstrikes against the North's command, communication, and nuclear assets.

North Korea had lost any hope of controlling the initiative. However, once it began, Pyongyang had no choice but to follow through. The Second Korean War had started.

By early March, South Korean soldiers had noticed the worst of the casting had worn off on the North Koreans, or perhaps those most affected were simply dead. Regardless, the suicide charges with sticks were replaced by a bloody defensive campaign until Kim Yo-jong's death six months later, shot by her own generals. The North surrendered, and unification was set to formally take place in 2045.

The war cost the lives of 1.4 million North Koreans, 225,000 South Koreans, and 3,500 Americans in just nine months. Luckily it never went nuclear and never escalated into a broader conflict with China.

The AMF was founded immediately after the war, but OpenCast use was almost non-existent on the Korean peninsula. The growth over the last few years had been great, but now it seemed to have stalled.

Globally, for the first time, there were open discussions in the media about ending Artemis's monopoly. Harbrinder sensed some real change in the air and doubled down on The Project, but the call for change gradually lost steam. Most of the general public, eventually even in Korea, just didn't seem to care enough as long as their coils worked. In the end, all that happened was the addition of another layer of bureaucracy, the World Casting Association.

Harbrinder stared into space, thought for a moment, and then decided to go grab some pizza on Grand Ave. He needed to clear his head before his next appointment, which was a personal one. Putting on his shoes, he stepped onto Merritt Ave. and then galloped down the Cleveland Cascade. There was a stream of people enjoying the weather as the late afternoon sun reflected off the flat water of the lake. He strode confidently down Lakeshore Avenue, his mind shifting to the upcoming cast. Last year, his therapist recommended using casting to experience empathy. He had experimented with this off and on before, but she suggested a more systematic approach. She told him to find a caster who specialized in empathetic subjects and attend the casts regularly. So he joined a weekly cast on the OpenNet called *The Journey* by a guy named David Ashbourne. David would "travel the world to capture the individual tragedies beneath the headlines." This week, he would be in Jakarta to cover the ongoing relocation efforts from rising sea levels.

Casting had unlocked whole new fields of therapy for mental health issues. A psychiatrist could not only prescribe casts as a form of therapy, but they could directly gauge a patient's issues through casting. For example, if you wanted to know how a patient was feeling, why not experience it directly?

Yet Harbrinder's area of concern, sociopathy, was still on the fringe of mental health research. The line between sociopathy and psychopathy, for example, was still poorly understood. They had found new names, like antisocial personality disorder, but relabeling it didn't take away the stigma. There was something about not caring for individual people that, in turn, made people not care for sociopaths. He understood. There were some bad sociopaths out there. He had noticed them lurking on the edges of the OpenNet. However, not all sociopaths were bad. Harbrinder, for his part, had no desire or need to hurt people. Really, he didn't even view his condition as a problem. There were advantages to being able to look at the world unemotionally without the cloud of individual attachment or guilt. In fact, back when he was a venture capitalist, he presumed most of his colleagues were also functioning sociopaths. Yet after he turned forty, he wondered if maybe it was time to share his life with someone. So he considered caring about caring and was lucky to have found a therapist who would take him seriously. He tried to follow her advice. Honestly, though, the results were mixed at best.

After lunch, Harbrinder walked back home, settled into a comfortable chair, and put on his OpenCast coil. He saw *The Journey* for this week had already begun. Clicking in, Harbrinder found himself in rubber waders, slowly trudging through waist-high water on what looked like a residential street. It was hot. David Ashbourne was emotionally disgusted and physically uncomfortable. Immediately around him was the floating detritus of a discarded society, while beneath uncertain feet was the stew that would not float.

"This is North Jakarta at high tide," Ashbourne said out loud. "A once vibrant part of the city that has been unraveling for over a decade. We've been invited to the home of a woman named Citra. Citra is the matriarch of her family. You can see her home coming up in front of us there."

Harbrinder felt the caster trudge toward a white two-story cinderblock structure on the corner of two small streets. All the single-story buildings nearby looked abandoned, but Citra's home and some of the other taller buildings still looked partially occupied. A sign for a clothing shop hung above the flooded ground floor. The downstairs doors and windows had all been removed. Inside floated two small plastic canoes.

As Ashbourne approached, he could see a small woman standing on the interior stairs. The details on her face were obscured by shadow, but her body language spoke of exhaustion. She motioned Ashbourne to come up the stairs.

Over the next hour, Citra described how she had grown up in this neighborhood, married, and spent her life running the clothing store and raising a family. She pulled out an old glass to show pictures, and Ashbourne relayed her pride to the audience. Then things started to fall apart. The flooding was a few times a year in the beginning. Then a few times a month. Now, you could only see the ground twice a day at low tide. The neighborhood was slowly destroyed, her business was lost, and her husband and sons left to look for work inland. Ashbourne felt each loss like it was his own. That was the cornerstone of his cast.

He was a natural empath, and Harbrinder felt it all through him, just like the rest of the audience.

The cast ended, and Harbrinder reached up to wipe a tear from his eye. He took a deep breath and checked his emotions. Perhaps a lingering concern for Citra? No, not really. It was gone moments after the cast ended. Instead, he started to feel bitter. Seeing the situation in Jakarta and the need for David Ashbourne to do these casts had left him in a foul mood. Jakarta should have been dealt with years ago. Why wouldn't people take action unless they were hit by their own empathy and guilt? Unless things were personalized through people like Citra? The old saying that the death of one man is a tragedy and the death of a million is a statistic still rang true.

Harbrinder put down his coil, stood up, and decided this empathy requirement was a weakness, not a strength. Why couldn't people do something just because it was the right thing to do? He was a goddamn sociopath, but he still knew right and wrong.

This would be his last edition of *The Journey*. He wasn't broken. He simply didn't need to feel guilty to do the right thing.

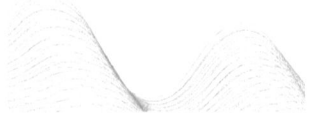

Peter & Katherine

P eter stepped out of the multi-rotor shortly after it touched down at
Artemis HQ. He waved goodbye to Jacob, the pilot, and walked
to the waiting AutoCab, smiling as he watched Jacob take off and head
back to Tiburon. He often wondered if Jacob really piloted when he was
on his own, or did he just hit the auto button? Passenger multi-rotors
were perfectly capable of autonomous flight, just like any other drone.
However, FAA regulations still required a butt in the seat. Peter thought
it probably had more to do with employment than safety.

The AutoCab took him the quarter mile to Building 12. He would
have preferred to walk, but that would have caused a scene with Artemis
employees. He missed the days of relative anonymity from a decade ago.
Nobody knew who he was back then, or if they did, he just got a wave,
like any normal human would.

He made the trip to check on the progress of the upcoming World
Casting Association Summit. The WCA was his ticket back to having
his own life, and he personally attended every major meeting. Katherine
Tanaka was handling the details, as usual, and he was heading to her
office. They could have just had a video call, of course, but this was
too important. And frankly, he wanted to see her. They had known
each other for over a decade, been through crisis after crisis together,
and their bond was deeper than just professional. His affection for her
was probably obvious to those around them, but he chuckled at rumors
that there was something more going on. The truth was Katherine

was like the daughter he never had. Besides, Peter truly loved and respected Linda. He had remained faithful through the years despite the temptations of his current status and her obsession with work. No reason to mess that up as he was, hopefully, on the homestretch to finally relaxing a little. He did worry about Katherine though. He'd never known her to have a steady love in her life.

"Hello, Sandra," Peter said as he walked into the lobby of Building 12. "How are things going here at the brain factory?"

"Peter!" Sandra yelped as she got up and came around the desk to give him a hug. "Things are great. Still having a lot of fun. The only thing missing around here is you."

"Well, give an old man a break, will you? I bet you'll be retired for a decade by the time you're my age."

"Oh no. Some of us have a bit more stamina for these things. I'll be here to shut the doors, just like I was here to open them."

"I bet you will. Say, Linda would love to see you. Why don't you come by the house for dinner tonight? You can take the multi-rotor back with me after my meetings."

"Sounds great, but some of us have busy social lives, you know. The Juniper Beetles are back in town, and that drummer still has the hots for me. I've been invited to see the show backstage, and then we'll see what else happens."

"Ha! Well, don't be out too late, young lady. You do have work tomorrow."

"Yes, sir!" Sandra said with a smile. "But I'd love to take a raincheck and come see you two. If it's okay, I'll ping your personal AI for a good night to come and reminisce."

"Please do. Or maybe we'll come over here and have some fun together. Anyway, I need to run upstairs, but I'll say goodbye on my way out if you're still here."

"You better. Now get up there and remind them all who's boss."

Peter walked over to the elevator, got in, and then held the door for the stunned people behind him.

"What floor for you guys?"

"F-Four . . ."

"Three for me, please, and it's a pleasure to meet you, sir."

"Pleasure is all mine. Now what departments do you two work in?"

Ninety seconds of small talk, then he was out onto the fifth floor and taking the short walk to Katherine's office.

"Knock, knock. Sorry for being late, you still free?"

"Peter! Absolutely, come on in. You know you do still have an office here. I'd be happy to come down to your space."

"Meh, we should get rid of that. I only come here to see VIPs like yourself."

They kissed each other on the cheek before Peter sat down in Katherine's guest chair.

"I'm assuming you'd like to know how things are coming for the summit?"

"I would indeed, but let's start with you. How are you doing?"

"I'm doing good, Peter. Work is still challenging, my parents are in good health, and I may have finally met someone who can put up with me," Katherine said with a smile.

"Oh, that's great to hear, Katherine. I do worry about you. I'm the last one who should be saying this, but work isn't everything."

"Yeah, we'll see how it goes. Still early days, but it's nice to have someone to look forward to seeing on the weekends."

"Well, if he breaks your heart, tell him he'll have to deal with me."

"I certainly will."

"And Frank? Is Frank treating you okay?"

"Oh yeah, Frank is fine. No problems there. In fact, he's showing more interest in the WCA lately as well."

"Oh really? How so?" Peter asked, a little surprised.

"Have you seen the latest numbers on the growth of Open-Cast/OpenNet?"

"I can't say that I have."

"Internal estimates say it's up to four percent of the traffic of the SmallNet. Not a lot in total, but it's been stuck at two percent for years."

"Huh, that is interesting. Any idea why?"

"Human Factors says the baseline two percent is your usual people on the fringe. Hardcore technologists who want to roll their own, nefarious actors, conspiracy theorists. However, they contribute most of the growth to getting around the advertising embeds."

"Really?" Peter couldn't help but smile. "Is it wrong of me to say good for them? Yes, that is probably wrong of me to say."

"Yes," Katherine smiled back. "That is wrong of you to say. You're forgetting how hacked together the OpenNet is. People can and do suffer serious trauma using OpenCast hardware and software."

"Well, can't you do some of your news stories through third parties on that? What was that one, Uzbeki prisons using the OpenNet with porn tags while torturing prisoners?"

"Yes, Peter, that was one of mine. And it worked. And it happens to be based on some truth. It happened at least once that we can verify."

Peter just smiled and looked at Katherine. He really did care for this woman. He hoped she would be happy someday.

"Well," Peter continued, "going back to Frank. What's his interest in the WCA again?"

"Right. I was getting to that. Frank thinks we should bring up the rise in OpenCast to the Ethics Committee. Remind them that they benefit from having one network with embeds that they can monitor. Remind them that every OpenCast is a percentage of the population out of their reach."

"Jesus, that does sound like Frank."

Peter was silent for a moment, trying to decide if he should tell Frank to fuck all the way off and get the hell away from his Ethics Committee or embrace the idea.

"Yeah, okay, we can do that," Peter decided. "We need all the leverage we can get to force the main players to standardize their Level 0 embeds. We can probably use OpenCast to rally around the flag a bit. I was planning on talking about how all these different rules in each geography were dragging Artemis down and preventing our network from being as effective as possible. In other words, we're not doing as well as we could with the Level 0 embeds without standardizing across geographies. If we add the threat of OpenCast in there, it is both the carrot and the stick. So sure, we can add that to the agenda."

"Help us be efficient against this common threat," Katherine said.

"Yeah, there you go," Peter agreed.

"Great, Frank will like that too."

"Yeah, that's fine," Peter said. "But look, my end goal here is to get a standard set of embeds and a standard process for submitting or removing embeds. It was all fine to replicate the US model with each government to start with, but in retrospect, where we messed up was in not having one model for everyone, period."

"Mmmm, that probably would have been too much to bite off back then."

"Maybe you're right. But what we have now doesn't scale and puts too much power in too few hands. In particular, my hands."

"Come on, Peter. You've done a great job. The world is in a good place."

"Not really. I mean, we are—you and I specifically, and perhaps most of the Western world generally. At least for the moment. But I think about all the people dead in Korea. God knows what's going on in China. Our Level 0 embeds are in place only because of a bunch of back-office deals that are hanging by a thread. I wonder if it was all worth it. And where will it go from here?"

"I think maybe you think too much," Katherine offered. "The world has always been a complicated place. Full of tragedy and grace, side by side. Right now, we have around nine billion people living on a single warming planet. The fact they haven't all tried to kill each other, at least not recently, probably has something to do with you. That alone is pretty amazing."

"You're too kind, as always. And I'm sorry, this conversation wasn't meant to be a pity-fest. Back to nuts-and-bolts. How does attendance look at the summit?"

"Good! We have confirmation for the General Session from all the delegates, including everyone on the Ethics Committee. Do you need any help putting your keynote together?"

"No," Peter said. "I mean, yes, after I finish the draft, I'll need help cleaning it up and maybe adding some data points. But I can get the first draft together. The keynote isn't a problem. They just expect me to say something about all the good stuff that comes from casting. Maybe a little about Artemis's charitable work. The usual boring crap. The important stuff will all be in the committees. A good summit for me will be getting a roadmap toward Level 0 standardization out of Ethics. If we can do that, I'll buy you a glass of champagne."

"Deal," Katherine said. "Now what else can I help you with?"

"You could show me where Jasper's office is these days. I promised I'd swing by and give him some shit for Linda," Peter said with a smile. "Love the guy, but his head is getting too big since he took over medical."

Katherine laughed and walked Peter down the hall while loudly saying, "Oh, Jasper? Jasper, my friend, I have a surprise for you!"

Jasper poked his head out of his office and made a big show out of running back in and shutting the door. Katherine hung around just long enough to share the laugh before heading back to her office.

★★★

Between Frank's request and Peter's agreement, Katherine had her marching orders with the Ethics Committee. Her Government Affairs team had overall responsibility for supporting the World Casting Association, however, she handled the Ethics Committee directly. There was only one member of the GA team that was even privy to the details of that committee. That was Jack Price, and frankly, Jack was only hired at the insistence of the US Government. It was an open secret that his loyalties were in Washington, DC. He was her own little in-house spy, keeping an eye on Artemis generally and senior staff specifically. Still, she enjoyed retaliating by having him do the grunt work, like booking conference rooms, arranging catering, and generally acting as a gopher when the delegates were in town.

The Ethics Committee itself consisted of the thirteen most powerful casting regions on the Artemis platform. The members were India, the United States, the European Union, the African Union, Japan, the United Kingdom, Indonesia, Australia, Mexico, Argentina, Canada, Brazil, and Saudi Arabia. The European Union currently held the rotating chair.

If you looked at the WCA website, you could see all the members and a charter to "Ensure casting was used for the betterment of humanity, including setting standards for ethical behavior in conjunction with the other Committees of the WCA. The Ethics Committee is an international resource for grievances arising from the use of casting within and across geographical boundaries."

All of this was true, and the Committee took its public role seriously. They viewed themselves as sheriffs in the Wild West of casting. However, the private function of the Committee was to help manage Level 0 embeds. Each of the members was one of the few thousand people around the world who had firsthand knowledge of Level 0 embeds. Each country had originally made its own agreement with Artemis for those embeds. Now the goal was to try to rationalize and standardize across regions. The separate Content and Consumption Committees were trying to do the same thing in their respective areas, albeit much more publicly.

Representing the EU and holding the chair was an Irishman named Michael Sullivan. Katherine made a point of maintaining a good relationship with all the committee members, and Michael was no exception. It was still early enough in Ireland to text and maybe even have a call.

"Hey, Michael—are you free for a call? If not, tomorrow would work."

"Katherine! It's always something interesting when you reach out. I'm free, and the suspense of waiting a day would kill me. Shall I call?"

"Thank you, yep, ready."

Michael's big, bushy face appeared on Katherine's dedicated video glass in her office. She couldn't help but think of Hagrid from the Harry Potter movies of her youth. Behind that big beard, Michael's mind was sharper than most, and she bet he would get right to the heart of the matter.

"Hello, Michael."

"Hello, yourself, Katherine. It's a pleasure to see you, but I'm assuming you have something to talk about."

"Thank you, Michael. Yes, we'd like to add something to the agenda for the upcoming meeting. A discussion around the dangers of the OpenNet."

"The OpenNet has been around for a while. What makes you want to discuss it now?"

"We are seeing a lot of growth there lately. Up to four percent of all SmallNet casting, which is double the norm. On the Artemis side, we would like to nip it in the bud. For all the countries in the WCA, it means an unregulated casting product in the wild. And for users, it represents a real danger."

"I'm not convinced four percent is a big deal," Michael said, "but if it continues to grow and we miss it, you'll never let me hear the end of it. So, sure, I guess we can use that open topics slot on Thursday. Sixty minutes?"

"That'd be great, thanks, Michael."

That done, she sent a note to Frank to confirm and knew Peter wouldn't leave without saying goodbye. She could tell him then.

Hmmm, it is Friday, Katherine thought with a smile. *Maybe I'll see if Harbrinder wants to come to the City tonight.*

Harbrinder & Katherine

H arbrinder still didn't know who this guy was, but he was obviously talented and possibly insane. It had been three weeks since that first message telling him to speed up his work, and this morning, the relationship got a lot more compelling.

He didn't even know what to call him. His username was *@johnofpatmos*. A quick search said it was an obscure biblical reference to the author of the Book of Revelations. Creepy. Harbrinder had replied simply enough to that first message.

@johnofpatmos: Speed up your work.

@hstrue: Why?

@johnofpatmos: Need an alternative platform.

@hstrue: Yeah, a lot of people agree with that. How do we speed up the work?

@johnofpatmos: Better, safer code. More trust.

@hstrue: There are a lot of people working on that. The code is open source. If you can contribute, feel free. Otherwise, we're trying.

Harbrinder didn't hear anything more and figured it was over. Then he received a message this morning from the OpenCast dev team that a new contributor had just dropped a significant rewrite of the Core OS. It ran demonstrably faster, but also claimed to have improved security and fail-safes. They were looking for Harbrinder's advice on what to do with the code. To accept it would mean a whole new branch of the OS, and they didn't know if they should spend the time analyzing it or just reject it wholesale. The contributor's username was *@johnop*.

Harbrinder recommended that the team take a serious look at the code—check it for any malware and make sure that the claimed improvements were real. If it all checked out, they'd take it for the gift that it was and see what they could do with it.

Hey, feel like giving me a ride home tonight?

Katherine. Nice. Of course he did.

You bet, come on over to the Blackfish *when you're ready. I'll book a guest slip in the City.*

Yet another gift, Harbrinder thought. This must be his lucky day. He got caught up on a few more messages, booked the guest slip, walked out of his house, and decided to do the five-kilometer loop around Lake Merritt. It was a pleasant Friday morning at the start of summer. Oakland enjoyed some of the best weather in the Bay Area, and today it was on full display. It rarely had the fog that enveloped San Francisco while still enjoying the impact of its natural cooling. The path around the lake was lined with hundreds of people enjoying the day, and Harbrinder was happy to join them. He had always loved being outside, whether sailing or simply taking a walk like this. He never understood people who stayed in all day, sitting in front of a glass in an office, seemingly isolated from the real world. Then going home and continuing the isolation there. He'd seen it his whole life. Everyone knew how unhealthy it was for both the body and mind. Still, people did it and did it by choice. It was like they were addicts with no self-control, and society did nothing about it. First, it was too much time in front of the television, then it was computers, then it was the internet and social media, and now it was casting. Each wave of technology more addicting than the last. For every person walking the lake right now, how many hundreds were castaways sitting in a room by themselves?

If it was up to Harbrinder, he would outlaw the technology altogether. That would never happen though, so he contented himself trying to at least negate the advertising influence through The Project.

He made it to the opposite side of the lake and decided to stop at the Lake Chalet for lunch. A lobster roll and beer sounded like a good way to celebrate the morning. He sat outside with the rest of the crowd and took in the sunshine. Then he saw it. Sitting at the far side of the patio was something he'd never seen here in Artemis's own backyard. There was a young man, dressed like a hipster, sitting with his friends wearing an OpenCast broadcasting coil. He couldn't help but stare. He'd never seen an Artemis coil of that design, so yes, it had to be an OpenCast coil. He smiled at this act of rebellion. A good chunk of the people around him were dependent on Artemis for their living in one way or another. Maybe this guy was just trying to be different or looking for shock value, but still, it warmed his heart. Humanity might not all be lost. He wondered if he should go up and talk to him? No, that would ruin it. He just ate his lunch and drank his beer. Harbrinder thought this day couldn't get any better.

He finished his walk, got undressed, and had another beer in the shower. He wasn't sure what Katherine had in mind tonight, so he dressed casually but put a change of clothes into an overnight bag, then called an AutoCab to take him down to the *Blackfish*. He chuckled again as the AutoCab pulled up. It happened to be one of his own. Most people, or at least most people who weren't wealthy, didn't really know how the whole AutoCab system worked, but Harbrinder wasn't too surprised to see his own AutoCab.

In the late 2020s, when autonomous driving finally started to take off, there were all these different systems competing with each other. As a user, you had to choose between different apps to get a ride. For example, in the SF Bay Area, you could choose between Waymo, Lyft, and Uber, just to name a few. And car manufacturers like Tesla and Mercedes had subscription services that allowed you to show up in one of their bespoke cars if you were willing to wait for a ride. However, the service that ended up dominating the space was from a latecomer called AutoCab. Founded by Tariq Khan, Tariq's genius was in the business model rather than the technology. Once all the other companies had done the hard work of getting the regulators on board and proving the technology, Tariq had purpose-built AutoCabs made first in Vietnam and later in North America and Germany. Then he simply treated them like the commodities they were. He offered the cabs to any investors who wanted to purchase ten, a hundred, or a thousand or more units. In return, AutoCab provided the end-user app, an autonomous safety check, an algorithm to recommend coverage locations, and liability insurance. Storage, charging, and maintenance were available for an additional fee. Larger operators like Harbrinder usually handled that themselves. Investors could depreciate the cost of the AutoCabs over six years while getting a steady return. Purchased in bulk, you would see an annual return of three to ten percent on cash depending on your service area. They were a hit with investors big and small. The cute little four-seat, purpose-built AutoCabs soon flooded multiple markets and became the dominant player. Now AutoCab was like Kleenex. Even if you used a different service, everyone still called it an AutoCab.

The genuine AutoCabs all looked similar. It was part of the branding. However, Harbrinder knew this one was one of his. The ID number on the side started with 36. Harbrinder had purchased a hundred AutoCabs through a subsidiary and had all the ID numbers start with a 36 in memory of his dad passing that year. He ran the cabs all around Oakland and Alameda. Every time a local Artemis employee got in one of his AutoCabs, they were funding OpenCast.

He was still smiling as he got out of the AutoCab at Jack London Square. He walked by The First and Last Chance Saloon on his way to the dock and figured "Why not?" He sat outside with another beer and watched the fashionable walk past.

His glass chirped.

"I should be there in an hour."

"No hurry. I'm here."

He attached a picture of his beer.

"Get a job. :)"

He typed, "You are my job" and then deleted it without sending. Instead, he sent, *"See you soon,"* finished his beer, and walked down to the *Blackfish.* He opened the companionway, took off the sail covers, and got the lines ready to run. It was a nice evening, and he was hoping Katherine would want to sail over instead of just motoring. She probably would. If she was in a hurry, they could have just taken the ferry.

Harbrinder grabbed another beer from the *Blackfish's* galley and sat in the cockpit, soaking in the late afternoon sun. He saw Katherine walking down the square toward the boat and gave her a wave as he got up to let her in through the gate. She was looking immaculately casual on a work Friday, and Harbrinder fully felt a lazy, spoiled, slightly drunk slob when he saw her. Walking to the gate, he cycled through something like true affection to resignation for the role he played with Katherine.

"Hey there, beautiful!"

"Hello, yourself! Already a few sheets to the wind, sailor boy?"

"Not too bad. In fact, maybe we can share a drink before we head out. You look like you could use one."

"I think I better stay dry until we get to SF. Isn't the Coast Guard usually busy in the estuary on a Friday afternoon? If we get boarded, I can say I'm in charge," Katherine said with a smile.

"That sounds like a good idea. In fact, why don't you really be in charge? You should take her over to SF, and I'll have another beer."

"Really?"

"Yeah, sure, why not. I'll be here watching. Why don't you take the helm, and I'll handle the rest for you."

"Okay, you're on. You do have insurance, right?" Katherine said with a chuckle.

"Never. You can't insure something that's priceless. You'll do fine."

Katherine climbed on board, still smiling. She'd seen Harbrinder maneuver the *Blackfish* enough times that she was excited to give it a try.

Harbrinder went below to turn on the instruments, grab a couple of lightweight coats, and find another beer.

"So, Captain Tanaka, let me show you the basics. Your rudder indicator is here. Start her out with the rudder right in the middle. Small adjustments from there. This lever down here is your throttle. Backward for reverse, middle for neutral, forward for forward. Again, small adjustments. I'll cast us off and then come back to keep an eye on you."

Harbrinder released the dock lines, and the *Blackfish* started to slowly drift between the two fingers of the slip. He stepped back into the cockpit, grabbed his beer, and leaned against the stern pulpit behind Katherine.

"Okay, ready when you are."

Katherine centered the wheel and slipped the 30kW motor into reverse. She gradually turned the wheel to port as the *Blackfish* slid silently into the marina fairway.

"Well done. Straighten her out, throttle to neutral. Great, now forward."

Katherine guided them into the body of the estuary. She smiled as the smell of food, people, and beer gave way to the brackish scent of the inner Bay.

"Good. Now give her a little juice to get us up around five knots. You can fall into line with the other outbound boats."

Harbrinder took up the fenders and stowed them in the lazarette. Then he grabbed one of the jackets, reached across Katherine, and hit the autopilot button.

"Here, let's put this on you, and then you can go back to the wheel."
Katherine put on the windbreaker, Harbrinder hit the standby
button to disengage the autopilot, and Katherine resumed control.

"This is fun. I thought it would be a little bit harder to steer."

"You're just lucky the *Blackfish* likes you. She makes it easy."

"Do you think we could sail over to the City?"

"Music to my ears, Katherine. It's pretty crowded tonight. We're
heading into the wind now, so we can raise the mainsail, but let's
hold off on really sailing until we clear the estuary."

Harbrinder made sure the halyard was on the winch, the sail ties
were off, and the lines were free to run. Then he reached across
Katherine again to get to the dedicated multifunction display in
the helm station and selected "full raise main" from the menu. The
electric winch kicked in, and the mainsail raised up from the boom.

They continued past the container ships at the entrance to the
estuary and tacked over toward the City. Harbrinder selected "jib
– 120%" and checked the "sail auto-trim" box. The *Blackfish* surged
forward while the Genoa deployed and trimmed itself. Harbrinder
turned off the electric motor and looked over to see Katherine smiling
broadly.

Harbrinder purposefully had the *Blackfish* slightly overpowered for
this wind. She was just starting to bury a rail, but the sail auto-trim
kept her from ever feeling out of control. The wind-driven sea state
in this part of the Bay was never too intense, and the *Blackfish* cut
smoothly through the water.

"Woohoo!"

"Woohoo, indeed. Let me know if you get tired, and I'll put her
on autopilot."

"No way. Now I understand why you do this."

"Just keep her pointed toward the Giants stadium. The guest slip is
there at the South Beach Harbor," Harbrinder said as he took another
sip of beer and smiled at Katherine.

Fifteen minutes later, they entered the vessel traffic area for the ferry service. Katherine could see one of the ferries exiting from San Francisco and accelerating toward them.

"Should I change course or anything?" Katherine asked.

"Nah. They'll clear us. Besides, look behind you."

Katherine turned and saw another ferry equidistant coming from the opposite direction.

"Oh dear."

"Yeah, you just gotta have faith in their autopilots. They are going much faster than us, and any change will only confuse them."

A few minutes later, the ferries simultaneously crossed ahead and behind the *Blackfish*, catching them in their wake from both sides.

"Shit," Katherine muttered, holding on tightly to the wheel as they were thrown about.

Harbrinder smiled, took another sip of beer, and said, "Exactly."

They hit the wind shadow on the City, and Harbrinder took over. He turned into the wind with the motor on and had the *Blackfish* automatically lower her sails. He hit the autopilot button, put the sail ties in place by hand, tied the fenders in place, and prepared the dock lines.

"There is a little bit of a crosswind at the dock, and parking can be tricky. I'll take her in."

Harbrinder brought them into the harbor and safely tied off at the dock.

"So, what's the plan tonight, Katherine? Should I change before we go to dinner?"

"Nope, I think you'll be fine. In fact, let's swing by my place, and I'll put on something more relaxed. There's a place in the Mission with a carnitas taco that I've been craving all week."

"Perfect."

As they started the fifteen-minute walk to Katherine's apartment, Harbrinder spontaneously reached out to hold Katherine's hand.

"Well done with the sailing, Captain Tanaka."

"Why, thank you, Captain Singh. You'll have to let me do that again."

"Absolutely."

They took the elevator up to her floor, and she unlocked the door with her glass. Harbrinder had seen her apartment before, of course, but it was always stunning to walk past the foyer, turn, and take in the view. Unlike purpose-built residential designs, the original office space floor plans didn't take into account the human need for natural light in the inner areas. That was just cube land, data centers, and break rooms. Converted buildings tried to make up for this issue by providing large open-floor plans. This didn't allow for much privacy, but it did provide dramatic views. The end result was that only one side of Katherine's two-thousand-square-foot apartment had windows, but those windows made up the entire wall. Her view from the fourteenth floor framed Treasure Island, the Bay Bridge, and much of the East Bay.

"I don't have any beer, but can I get you a glass of wine?"

"That would be great, thank you."

Katherine opened a bottle of white wine and got out two glasses.

"I don't think I can catch up to you, but I will join you now that we're on dry land."

"Cheers." Harbrinder took the glass and leaned in for a kiss, which Katherine provided.

"Now, drink your wine while I change, then you can buy me a taco."

"Deal," he said as he sat down in an overstuffed chair.

Katherine stepped into the bedroom, one of the few enclosed spaces in the apartment, but left the bedroom door open as she unselfconsciously changed into jeans and a sweater.

Harbrinder caught glimpses of Katherine as they continued their small talk. *Yep,* he thought to himself, *this is a great day.*

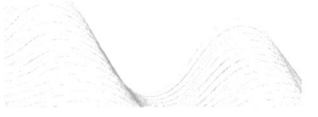

Henry

H enry was confident the OpenCast devs would take his code. There would be bugs in it, he knew, but the code was good. A generation ahead of what they already had in both performance and security.

He wasn't sure at first how it would feel to submit the build. He was afraid it would feel like he was stealing from Artemis or betraying Peter, but it didn't feel like that at all. In fact, it felt good. He wrote most of the original Level 1 code at Artemis anyway, and this new code was tweaked enough to be considered unique. There were also one or two good ideas in the original OpenNet OS that he kept around.

It was in the Level 0 hooks and embeds that the code had the most resemblance to Artemis. He didn't bother to change those much at all. Again, he had written most of that code to begin with, and it wasn't stealing advertising money from Peter. But most importantly, he knew it worked and was virtually undetectable. Years of Artemis's OS devs and Level 1 security personnel had yet to detect it, so he didn't think the open-source devs would either.

Still, there was a chance it could be found. So Henry decided not to place any active embeds until the code was accepted. If the ability to place embeds was discovered, he could always claim it was a bug. After the core code was accepted, he would then wait until the first dot release to introduce embeds.

Henry gave a lot of thought to what the embeds should be. He figured the first ones would be easy, he would just duplicate Peter's First Two.

- "Helping each other is good"

- "Theft is bad"

He knew these really, really well. He could set up his own AI to do the execution for now, the call hidden in the shared secret request built into the Level 1 security. He would probably need to throw more power at it over time, but he didn't need anything close to Harpo's size. The user group was much smaller, and there weren't any conflicting rules across geographies he had to worry about. The OpenNet metatags were almost useless, but he would bias the embeds even further toward subtlety to be safe.

Henry decided he would keep it to these two embeds for months. Just let it run and look for patterns. Then he could introduce the rest of the Ten Commandments gradually over time. He figured he would do it in reverse order as they appeared in the Bible. He was looking forward to the first one he would do, the Tenth Commandment, "Thou shalt not covet." This was the antithesis of all the Level 2 embeds at Artemis. He liked that. He also knew that getting away from consumerism was why a lot of people joined the OpenNet to begin with. He was sure that one would go well.

Henry knew it would take years to gradually introduce all Ten Commandments. Some of the embeds would be tricky to write. Some of them may cause behavior changes that would bring the OpenNet under scrutiny. All of it seemed like a very interesting puzzle to Henry and the most important thing he could possibly do with his time.

He looked over at the print of the Ten Commandments that he kept framed on the wall. Yes, he would do the tenth one next. After that, the others were:

9 – *"Thou shalt not bear false witness against thy neighbor."*

He wondered if he should just make this one "Don't lie" or maybe "Don't lie about important things."

8 – "Thou shalt not steal."

Taken care of with "Theft is bad."

7 – "Thou shalt not commit adultery."

This one would be a challenge. Henry would have to decide if receiving a pornographic cast while married was adultery. He might need to talk to his pastor about it, which would make Henry uncomfortable. If he decided it was adultery, it would really change the OpenNet and potentially reveal some level of manipulation. Also, Henry didn't like all the bad sexual things on the OpenNet, but it wasn't really covered by the Ten Commandments. He may need help from the rest of the Bible.

6 – "Thou shalt not kill."

Peter said the government didn't like this one, but Henry was happy to include it. He thought he would change it to "Murder is bad."

5 – "Honor thy father and thy mother."

Another easy one, although Henry admitted not honoring his father very much. This was a good reminder that he should try.

4 – "Remember the Sabbath day, to keep it holy."

This one would be hard. It might be noticed if most OpenCast users suddenly started going to church. He would probably have to introduce it gradually.

3 – "Thou shalt not take the name of the Lord thy God in vain."

This one was more involved than it looked. Henry could just make it "Don't say bad things about God" or he could make it into something bigger. Something like "Don't say mean things" or even "Don't say anything God wouldn't like." He would have to pray on this one.

2 – "Thou shalt not make unto thee any graven image."

Henry liked this one. He felt it meant "Always put God first," and that was just what he was doing. As much as he liked this one, it would be complicated to deploy and not be noticed. Hopefully, he would learn some lessons from the Fourth Commandment.

1 – "Thou shalt have no other gods before Me."

This one would be the hardest, and he knew it was smart to save it for last. He could make it easy on himself and pretend it was like the Second Commandment. Always put God first. That could be whatever God you decided it was. However, Henry knew in his heart that he couldn't do that. He knew it didn't mean that. He knew that Jesus Christ was the Lord God made manifest on Earth and that there was no other God before Him. He needed to get that message out. He would have to think and pray on how to do it, but he knew that it would be the culmination of his life's work.

God had made Henry different for a reason, and now he knew why.

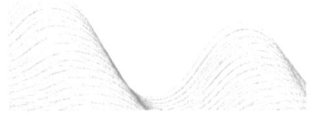

Harbrinder & Katherine

Harbrinder was awake but didn't want to open his eyes. Doing so would acknowledge his existence. His mouth felt like a cotton ball soaked in diesel, his bladder was full, and the slightest movement of his head was pain. He decided the best thing to do was to ignore it all and feign sleep.

"Morning, Sunshine."

He cracked open an eye. A needle of pain cut deep into his brain. He caught the outline of a woman—Katherine, he supposed—holding a cup of tea. He shut his eyes.

"Tequila got your tongue?"

At the mention of tequila, Harbrinder threw back the covers and slowly began to put his feet on the ground. His entire body rejected the idea, but laying back down would mean puking on her bed instead of someplace better.

"No offense, but you looked a lot sexier last night," Katherine said.

Harbrinder moaned, got up, stumbled to the bathroom, and shut the door behind him. He stood over the toilet with his hand on the wall, trying to decide if he should puke or pee first. He was already standing, so peeing won.

Emptying his bladder freed his mind enough to take inventory of the damage he'd done. Beer. Lots of beer. Some wine at her apartment. More beer and two shots of tequila with tacos. Another glass of wine back at her apartment. Stupid.

He resisted the urge to puke and turned on the faucet, alternating between washing his face and drinking cupped handfuls. He risked a glance in the mirror and quickly looked away. Katherine had a bottle of hydrogen peroxide mouthwash on the counter. No alcohol. Good. Harbrinder took a swig and swished it around. Still avoiding the mirror, he spit it out, rinsed his mouth, and stepped back into the bedroom.

Harbrinder reached the edge of the bed, sat down, and tried to sit up straight. Katherine was still standing there with a mug of tea in her hand and a smirk on her face.

"Coffee?" Harbrinder said.

"Just tea at home, I'm afraid. We can go out and get you some coffee if you feel up for it."

"Need coffee," Harbrinder replied.

Katherine walked out of the bedroom and returned a few minutes later.

"Here, it's green tea. Maybe this will revive you enough to go get coffee."

Harbrinder took the mug without saying a word. The smell didn't completely turn his stomach. He ventured a sip.

"Hot," was all he said.

"Yes, very good, sweetie. It's hot."

Harbrinder felt a flicker of annoyance at the sarcasm, but then he remembered the more pleasant moments from last night. He supposed she was entitled to some teasing at his expense.

"Thank you for the tea," Harbrinder said while still looking down at his mug.

"You are welcome. Take your time and recover. I'm going to get caught up on a few things in the next room. Let me know when you're ready to join the living."

Five minutes and half a mug of tea later, Harbrinder decided to try moving. He managed to pull on his pants and wrinkled shirt before slumping back down on the bed. The effort of dressing exhausted him. He was stuck between not being able to sleep and barely functioning. Nothing left to do but try to move forward.

He walked out into the living room. Katherine sat on the couch, tapping away on her glass, and didn't look up as he sat down on the chair opposite her.

The silence lingered in the air between them for a few moments before Katherine said, "So, should we get you that coffee and maybe a little something in your stomach?"

"I'm willing to try anyway," Harbrinder said.

They took the elevator down to Fremont St., and Katherine led them toward the Embarcadero. The fresh air hit Harbrinder's face like a kiss from an angel. He had no idea how much he needed that. He just might live after all.

They walked along the waterfront in relative silence toward the Ferry Building. The Embarcadero was full of people enjoying a Saturday morning. Harbrinder felt his strength gradually returning.

Approaching the south entrance to the Ferry Building, Katherine said, "There's a breakfast spot in here that I think you might like."

Harbrinder nodded his assent, and they stepped inside. The main hall was packed with people shopping at various stands or waiting for a table. They were a hundred paces in when they approached a restaurant facing the water. Katherine asked the hostess for a table for two.

"It'll be about fifteen minutes," Katherine said as she returned to Harbrinder's side.

"Fine," he muttered, but the enclosed space and crowds had brought the nausea back. "Do you think we could wait outside?"

"Umm, sure, I'll ask them to ping my glass when ready."

Katherine returned, and they walked outside. Harbrinder leaned against the railing of the dock and was once again saved by the fresh air.

"Boy, you really did it to yourself last night, didn't you?"

"Yeah, that was a mistake. I guess I felt like celebrating and overdid it a bit."

"Celebrating? I didn't even know we were celebrating. What were we celebrating?"

Harbrinder almost fell back into his role by saying, "Seeing you," but paused. Maybe it was the hangover, but he didn't feel like playing the game right now. Instead, he said, "Why do you keep working at Artemis? I mean, you don't really have to work anymore. So why do you keep doing it?"

"Wow," Katherine replied. "I would have expected a question like that last night after a few drinks. Shouldn't you at least have your coffee before asking things like that?"

Harbrinder looked into Katherine's eyes and could see she was genuinely taken by surprise. He felt like pressing the issue, but Katherine wasn't wrong. He probably should have his coffee first. He was saved as Katherine's glass pinged. "Table's ready," she said.

They walked back inside and were led through the crowded restaurant to a table on the patio. They sat down, and Katherine asked for two coffees.

"You going to be okay sitting out here?"

"Yeah, I think so. The fresh air helps."

The coffee came, and Harbrinder looked over the menu. It was a fashionable restaurant with real printed menus and a human waitstaff. You had to verbally ask for things instead of just tapping on your glass. *Maybe a breakfast sandwich will help*, he thought. He took a few sips of his coffee, and Katherine said, "I like it, you know."

"Hmmm, like what?"

"I like the work. I like the people, and I feel like it's important work."

Harbrinder took another sip of his coffee and looked out onto the Bay. "But what are you working towards? Making casting more popular?"

Katherine glanced at the tables around her before responding.

"Making responsible casting more popular, sure," she said quietly.

"You feel Artemis is responsible casting?"

"Yeah, I do. It is well-regulated and proven safe. What's the alternative? The People's Network in China? Whatever the heck is coming out of Russia? The wasteland that is OpenCast?"

Harbrinder stared down at his menu and thought about how far to take this. He not only wanted to have this argument, but he wanted to win it. It wasn't about justifying his own work. He wanted to bring Katherine along with him.

"OpenCast seems like a reasonable alternative, don't you think? No advertising at least."

"No, I do not," she said with a slight shake of her head. "You don't see the things that I see about OpenCast. People have suffered from both hardware issues and traumatizing content. Anarchy is not the answer."

"Not sure forcing people to consume advertising is the answer either."

"People can pay for the ad-free version if they want."

"So it's okay to brainwash people if it only impacts the poor?"

The waitress walked up and interjected, "Hi there, can I answer any questions about the menu or do you two know what you want?"

Katherine and Harbrinder stared at each other for a moment before Harbrinder looked up at the waitress. "I'll have the breakfast sandwich, a glass of orange juice, and a refill on the coffee, please."

"Hmmm, my wealthy boyfriend here is paying, so let's see. Looks like the truffle omelet is the most expensive thing on the menu. I'll have that, with, oh, a glass of Dom Perignon, please."

Harbrinder smiled at the sarcasm and looked at Katherine. She was an amazing woman, intelligent and opinionated, which was why he wanted to bring her over to his line of thinking.

Katherine stared back at Harbrinder as the waitress walked away. "Look, Robin Hood, making sure advertising is well regulated is precisely why good people need to stay involved. It's why we work with the government. It's why we support the World Casting Association."

"The problem is that Artemis has a profit motive to keep advertising," Harbrinder said. "Maybe they change what's advertised, but the advertising stays regardless. And yes, despite my own financial status, I do think it's unfair that advertising impacts those that can least afford it."

"Again, that's why both regulation and robust personas are so important. So we don't advertise Porsches to people making minimum wage. But it sounds like what you're really complaining about is capitalism? Kind of ironic coming from you, isn't it?"

"No, not complaining about capitalism. I'm complaining about taking away people's free will."

"That's also an argument as old as civilization," Katherine said. "There's always an impact to individual free will any time you engage with society. You could be talking about the church, the government, a trade union, mass media, your local bar, a family reunion, it doesn't matter. If you're going to participate in a social construct, there will always be an impact to individual free will. That's the price of admission. Want true free will? Go be a hermit."

"Casting is a little different than a family reunion."

"Yeah, I would argue casting has less of a long-term impact psychologically than a family reunion. Nitpicking aside, all media does, all any media does, is scale existing social constructs. That's how communication works. There has to be a shared reference point, and someone has to frame the discussion. It doesn't matter if it's the government controlling the media, or a for-profit company, or just an individual expressing a point of view. If the communication is successful, there will still be an impact to free will. Even in this discussion, we are trying to impact each other's free will on a topic by communicating."

"I'm having this discussion with you out of genuine interest and even compassion. That's the difference. Companies driven by a profit model don't give a crap about the individual."

"But they do give a crap about the collective 'customer,' don't they? They want to keep them around and wealthy enough to keep consuming. Look at what happened in Korea. Did that explode because the North Koreans were busy advertising Coca-Cola? No. Personally, I think a hybrid model with private companies under government regulation is probably the best we can do. Some sort of check and balance. At least in the case of Artemis casting, you have regulatory bodies to complain to, like the WCA."

"You mean like that Ethics Committee you mentioned? Not sure they really do much."

"They do more than you realize."

"Really?" Harbrinder said. "Like what?"

"I don't know, I'm not directly involved," she said. "But the point is that at least there's someone to complain to. In the OpenCast model, after you've been traumatized by selecting a violent cast, who are you going to call?"

"It's true that with freedom comes risk. In this case, the freedom of OpenCast comes with the risk of a bad cast. However, compare that to the certainty that a cast will manipulate you by advertising and that your only recourse is to complain to a bureaucracy that, oh, by the way, is endorsed by the same system that just manipulated you."

The tension floated above the table as the food came out. The waitress put the food down and looked silently back and forth between them. She walked away unacknowledged.

"Look," Katherine said, "I know you have strong opinions, but trust me, I am working with some good people. Peter and Linda are only trying to do what's best."

"I do trust you, Katherine, but who elected Peter and Linda to determine what's best for the rest of us?"

"I like my job, Harbrinder. You may want to consider getting one someday. Then you might know what it's like to make tough decisions."

"Tough decisions? Yeah, I made the tough decision not to harm people with my work."

Katherine stared icily at Harbrinder. Her teeth were grinding, and she held her knife and fork like weapons.

Okay, Harbrinder thought, *I've taken this as far as it will go today.* "How's the champagne and truffle omelet?"

"The omelet is good." Katherine picked up the champagne and poured it into Harbrinder's orange juice. "The champagne was for you. You seem to need it more than I do."

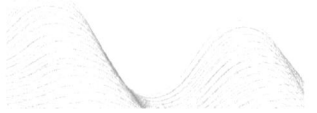

Frank

F rank sighed as he retrieved his eggs from the hotel's AutoChef and went looking for some hot sauce. He had been in India for less than a week and had already gotten used to idli, sambar, and a Mysore dosa for breakfast. After decades of working in the Bay Area's biotech industry, he had developed a taste for Indian food. Getting a chance to eat it every day was hands down his favorite part of any trip to India. Now he was stopping over in New York for a day on his way back to Alameda, eating automated food from the hotel restaurant while he waited for Adam Ricci, Senior Vice President of East Coast Sales, to join him.

The trip had been a mixed bag so far. Uganda went pretty much as expected. No surprises from the local team and plenty of footage of him meeting with Ugandan volunteers. They even had one of them casting out the meeting from their perspective. He heard the caster was sending out genuine excitement and gratitude for being part of the event. A risky play by the local PR team, but he'd be sure to tell Katherine how well it went.

In India, the food was the only good part of the trip. Raj's reasons for missing deadlines appeared to be caused by mismanagement instead of legitimate obstacles. The guy was given plenty of resources and free reign to align them as he saw fit, so Frank had little patience for the excuses. The worst thing was Raj being openly incredulous that Frank would even question their processes. Unfortunately, it looked like Raj had fallen prey to his own ego and built a little empire of sycophants. It might be time to isolate the local AI and do some house cleaning through a couple of layers of management, which would certainly delay things further. Raj had also done a lot of ass-kissing with the Indian government and built up a base of support there. Frank would probably need to work with the Government Affairs team before making a move. Still, better to get it done sooner than later. Otherwise, the problem would just continue to grow deeper and deeper through the ranks. Frank sat down at a table and stared down at his omelet. It's a good thing he liked Indian food—he would be spending more time there in the near future.

He saw Adam enter the dining room and stood up to wave him over and shake his hand.

"Hey, Adam, good to see you."

"Great to see you, Frank. Thanks for making the time."

"No problem at all. I wanted to get your thoughts directly before we head into the office and see the rest of the team. Did you want to grab a bite to eat?"

Adam glanced down at Frank's plate and said, "Maybe just coffee."

"Smart man."

Adam walked over to the coffee station, and Frank sat down again to finish off his omelet. As he returned, Adam asked, "How's the trip going?"

"Pluses and minuses. Happy to break up the return trip with a visit to New York. How's the team doing?"

"Good, overall. The usual complaints, which we can talk about, but I don't think you'll be too surprised by the questions you'll hear."

"Let me guess—they want to know when the restrictions will be lowered on the intensity and subjects that can be advertised?"

"Bingo! You know this, but they see a lot of money being left on the table. Luxury goods want to advertise at lower economic levels to build a pipeline of demand and brand awareness. Food, beverage, and service vendors say they'll pay more to increase the intensity. Not to mention the alcohol and cannabis vendors just wanting to get in the door to begin with."

"Sure, but hasn't the team thought through the next step? I mean, if the restrictions were eased, don't they know I'm just going to raise their quotas?" Frank said with a smile.

"You know these guys only think quarter to quarter, Frank," Adam replied jokingly.

"Speaking of which," Frank continued, "you barely made your numbers last quarter, which is unusual for you. Want to give me your thoughts on that?"

"I do. As you know, we have good insight into what our customers are willing to spend every year and can map that into the expected numbers and types of casts. Outside of any large macro disruptions, like when Korea hit, we can predict any given quarter pretty damn well. On top of that, like any good sales leader, I keep a few things in reserve, just in case. Y'know, like a percentage or two of total sales."

"Yeah, sure. Everyone does that in their regions, and then at my level, I push or pull to hit our overall numbers while trying to keep something in the tank. I remember pushing you guys last quarter and not getting much out of it."

"It's true, Frank. That's the thing. I pulled out all my reserves and barely made the numbers. The team feels it as well, and that's why there's a renewed push for fewer restrictions. They're willing to fight but don't want to do it with one hand tied behind their back. But you know what, I was saying the same thing back when I was an account manager. Between you and me, I don't think the restrictions are the big issue. They're not exactly something new. I think there is something else going on."

"Mmmm, do tell?"

"It's not a demand issue, Frank. I have a backlog of customers who want to sponsor casts. I think it's a supply issue."

"You're talking about the number of casts available?"

"Don't get me wrong, casting is obviously still in a growth mode, but it's starting to slow. I think growth expectations, and our quotas are a percent or two off from reality. Not a lot, but enough to cause me to pull in my backlog for now and, God forbid, risk actually missing a our number in the future."

"So you want me to lower your quota?"

"The number of casts is what it is," Adam said with a shrug. "If you want nine percent more revenue on eight percent more casts, then we need to look into other options. Maybe we can get the restrictions loosened to allow multiple ad embeds in a stream? Or get other restrictions eased and charge a premium for first mover access? Or how about simply raising prices? If you don't like any of those options, help me get more casts for my customers. Ask Marketing to subsidize more BigNet casts in my region. Otherwise, every quarter is going to be a struggle."

"Well, I'm not going to lower your quota," Frank said, "but you knew that. Maybe there is something we can do on the fringes of pricing, but I won't support anything that kicks off customer complaints to the FTC. And the restrictions are what they are. We aren't going to get a lot of sympathy from the government for being really profitable instead of obscenely profitable. To complicate things further, the WCA is meeting next month. We might see some changes in regulations coming out of that in the future."

"You really think the US government will allow the WCA to set guidelines?"

"It will take a year or two to implement, but yes, I do. Especially for international casts. Don't get me wrong, the US will negotiate within the WCA, and I'm sure there will be cut-outs and loopholes, but it's all in lockstep with global trade agreements anyway. This is just the natural next step linking the two. Anyway, that's in the future. We'll see how that impacts your quotas when it happens."

"Interesting. So how about some help from Marketing for some BigNet casts?"

"You can talk to Susan and see if she can help, but her budget is fixed for the year, and you know all your peers will be asking her for the same thing. So feel free to try, maybe she has some discretionary funds, but I'm not going to override Susan. You're on your own there."

"All right, Frank. Well, I won't pretend that I'm surprised by your answers. Still, the root of my issue is that the casts available to sell are slightly below forecasts. The team is executing as always, but those forecasts need to be more accurate if compensation is going to be tied to them."

"You know the AIs and people making those forecasts are the best we have, but still, that's a fair comment. In fact, I have a theory that might account for the discrepancy."

"Oh, yeah."

"Yeah, let me know if this sounds crazy, but have you seen any extra OpenCast activity lately?"

Adam frowned slightly. "OpenCast? Sure, I guess so. But all casting is growing. I just figured OpenCast was growing in step."

"No, the absolute numbers are still relatively small, but there is some data suggesting that OpenCast growth is consistently outpacing the SmallNet."

"Wow—that is interesting."

"Yeah, again, the overall numbers aren't huge, but it might explain why the forecasts are off by a percent or two. It might account for some of the pressure you're feeling."

"Huh. Now that you mention it," Adam said, "there was this one story I heard from a junior outside sales guy on our team. I guess there's a popular ramen place over on West 53rd that he likes to go to. Anyway, the chef there walks around the whole time wearing an OpenCast broadcasting coil. Apparently, thousands of people like to tune in while this guy is just making noodles. So our sales guy tells him that if he's going to do that, he should put it on the SmallNet and at least make some money. There are plenty of food and beverage vendors that would love to sponsor something like that. But I guess this chef was all zen about it. He said it wasn't about the money, it was about the noodles, and he left it there. Some of his followers were watching the whole exchange, and I guess this guy is now a big OpenCast hero. It seemed just like a funny story at the time."

"Seems like there might be enough of these stories to make a dent," Frank said.

"Okay, well, does the company have a plan for taking care of it?"

"Maybe," Frank said. "We'll see after the WCA meeting."

Harbrinder

A week had passed since the argument with Katherine. She had walked him back to the *Blackfish* after breakfast. He knew his lack of empathy sometimes got him into trouble, but Harbrinder felt they were on good enough terms as they parted. There was a dinner together mid-week. No more talk about her work. Yet there was no denying that it was Saturday, and Harbrinder was home alone. No invitation to the City. When he had gently brought up the idea, she said she had a lot of work to catch up on and maybe next weekend. So, yeah, he had hit a nerve, but he had a hard time regretting it. To his amazement, he wanted her approval. If he was going to bring her around to his point of view, he had to start the process at some point. He felt like her defensiveness on the subject was a good sign. It was just how someone who had inner doubts might act.

Having the weekend free wasn't all bad. He had his own work to catch up on. Tomorrow he was supposed to conduct a top donor tour at the Singh Animal Shelter. Always tedious, always predictable, but he did it out of respect for his late father. He would walk a group of wealthy-ish people, usually older women and their grandchildren, through the shelter and talk about the responsibility to be kind to all of God's creatures. There would be noise. There would be the smell of urine and feces. He would explain how they were a no-kill facility. He would show them the medical facilities where animals were cared for if needed and where all were neutered or spayed. He would get the same questions at the end, including, "How many pets do you have?" And he would give the same answers, including, "These are all my pets." By the end of the tour, at least one or two animals would be adopted by a spoiled kid or lonely lady. Harbrinder would thank everyone while standing next to a glass scanner that said, "Donations welcome." Everyone would smile and tap their glass on the way out.

Privately, Harbrinder had always found the animals locked in cages to be depressing. Some of them would live the rest of their lives like that simply because they weren't charismatic enough to be adopted. Then there were the other ones who would stop eating until they were discreetly put down out of mercy. The staff did their best, but still, it was depressing. Not that he ever wanted to take any of them home. That wasn't who he was. He just thought most of them should be neutered and set free. Let them roam. Better to die free than to live in a cage.

All that was for tomorrow. Today, he had more important work. The OpenCast dev team had completed their initial review of the Core OS rewrite from @johnofpatmos and were impressed. Some bugs to work out, but clearly a step above the existing code. They recommended adopting it as a major version release and exposing it to the broader community for further analysis and development. The devs had the power to make that decision on their own, but he asked them for the weekend to look into a couple of things.

The devs didn't know how long @johnofpatmos had been working on the code. From their perspective, he may have been preparing this release for years. Harbrinder, on the other hand, had a feeling that the code had been put together in a matter of weeks. Specifically since his last direct interaction with @johnofpatmos. How would someone put together a significant improvement to a major OS in a matter of weeks, even with the help of an AI? Harbrinder could only think of two options. The first option was an existing member of the OpenCast dev community who had previous experience with the OpenCast Core OS. That seemed highly unlikely. Too much new code, and those devs wouldn't hide behind a new persona to deliver this amount of work. They would want to take credit for it. The second option was the developer had experience with another casting OS. The only other major casting OSs were from Artemis, China, and Russia. He could rule out the Russian one. If their OS was this good, they would have heard about it. China was a possibility, he supposed. He didn't have a lot of experience with their platform, but China would likely benefit from weakening Artemis's grip. However, the most likely conclusion was that he was dealing with an Artemis insider. Perhaps a disgruntled employee. Which could be a gold mine or a legal disaster if Artemis went after OpenCast for stealing code. He decided to see if he could get more info from "John."

@hstrue: *Hey, thank you for that code drop. It's impressive, but I'm not sure we can use it.*

@johnofpatmos: *Why?*

Hmm, that was a pretty quick response for a Saturday and there was no denial that he dropped the code.

@hstrue: *I'm concerned that there may be proprietary code in there. Looks like something that could have come from a professional outfit, like maybe Artemis.*

There was a delay of over a minute before he responded again.

@johnofpatmos: *It's my code. I wrote it. It will make OpenCast better. You need to use it.*

@hstrue: *You seem anxious to make OpenCast better. Why?*

@johnofpatmos: *Need an alternative to Artemis.*

@hstrue: *Yes, again, a lot of people feel that way. But you haven't said why you want an alternative to Artemis. It's hard for me to trust what you're doing if I don't know your motives. You might end up getting us in legal trouble.*

A longer delay.

@johnofpatmos: *The World Casting Association may do some bad things. People need an alternative.*

@hstrue: *You mean with advertising and the Consumption Committee?*

Another delay.

@johnofpatmos: No, not that. You need to look into the Ethics Committee.

@hstrue: Why? Are you afraid they'll block you from doing something illegal?

@johnofpatmos: You need to look into the Ethics Committee.

Now it was Harbrinder's turn to pause. He remembered Katherine mentioning the Ethics Committee a couple of times. What did she say at breakfast? *"They do more than you realize." Shit, what do they do?* Maybe this guy John was right. Maybe he needed to look into it more. But he still didn't know if he should trust him.

@hstrue: Look, that is interesting and maybe I do need to look into it more, but again, I don't know who you are and if we can trust what you're saying.

No reply for several minutes while Harbrinder digested the exchange. He was just getting ready to move on to other things when a new message came in.

@johnofpatmos: 1 file attached

Harbrinder recognized the file type as an Artemis brain scan. The same type of HIPAA-controlled document that was the basis for both Artemis and OpenCast coils. He opened it with a viewer and read the metadata.

Singh, Harbrinder

SSN: XXX-89-5489

Jesus, this guy just sent him his own brain scan. Had he been hacked? He thought back to his use of the document. He had a copy on his personal AI, he'd shared a copy with one of the OpenCast devs years ago when he made his first OpenCast coil, and then of course Artemis had a copy. His messenger dinged again.

@johnofpatmos: 1 file attached

It was a plain text file. The first lines read:

America's Cup Race 7

Broadcasting Location: Valencia, Spain

Date: 05/06/2041

Duration: 1hr 57m 32s

Ad-free subscription service

And then it continued on with the history of the Artemis casts he had watched. Not a lot of them. The America's Cup last year was the last time he was willing to use their system. However, further down the list were some casts he preferred not to be public. Chalk it up to research.

@hstrue: OK, you've got my attention. You obviously have access to confidential information. However, if you're willing to steal this information, how do I know you didn't steal the code you sent us?

@johnofpatmos: I did not steal this information. This is your own information that I also have access to. No theft. The code I sent was my code. No theft. Theft is bad.

A short pause.

@hstrue: I'll look into the Ethics Committee. Please send more details if you can.

No response.

Harbrinder spent Saturday night home alone, thinking through his next steps over a glass or two of whisky. He was now confident John was an Artemis employee. There was no other realistic option. Seemed like he was a fairly senior one at that. What would freak out an Artemis employee so badly that they would take this risk? What was this Ethics Committee doing? Katherine said she wasn't involved, but she obviously knew something was going on. What he really needed was to get to someone directly on the committee.

On Sunday morning, he woke up and made a strong pot of coffee. Then he sent two messages. The first was to the OpenCast devs recommending a hold on the broader release of the new OS for now. He also recommended doing a scrub for proprietary code, specifically Artemis code. The second message was to Katherine. *"Lunch this week?"*

Katherine

"*Sure. How about one o'clock on Wednesday at Mint Leaf?*" Harbrinder wanted to go to lunch. Fine. She would give him a chance, but he certainly pissed her off last weekend. Drinking all day and then having the nerve to question what she was doing with her life as he sat there hungover and semi-comatose. Honestly, it felt like another relationship starting to fall apart. Why did he have to try to make her work sound evil? Is he just trying to bring me down because of his own insecurities? What did he expect her to say? "*Wow, I guess you're right. I'll quit my job and day drink with you instead.*"

Katherine was self-aware enough to know she pushed people away in her personal life by being too sensitive. So she would talk with Harbrinder, but with the WCA meeting coming up next month, she was way too busy to baby him. He'd have to accommodate her schedule. Unlike Harbrinder, she had a job to do.

Monday morning came, the week began, and the alarm went off at 5:45 a.m. Katherine was jolted awake. It had been a rough night of sleep, and she had finally dozed off only an hour earlier. Still, she kept her routine: get dressed and get out for her run before she came back to shower and review the news feed from Suzi over breakfast. Then she'd walk down to the ferry and review messages on the trip to Alameda.

She sighed as she looked out the window and watched Yerba Buena Island pass by. One of her overnight messages was from Barbara Taylor, the casting representative for Australia and the current chairwoman of the WCA. The Committee Chairs all owned their own breakouts, while Barbara's team owned the overall schedule for the summit. Katherine's Government Affairs team was downstream from all of them, providing support where needed. That support could be anything from answering detailed technical questions, to providing analytics, to getting donuts. The arrangement was perfectly logical, but Barbara had a tendency to come off as condescending to any Artemis employee, including Katherine. Where Katherine could look at someone like Michael Sullivan on Ethics as a partner, Barbara treated Katherine as a subordinate. Her message this morning was typical.

Katherine,

Use the link included to view the latest agenda. Your actions in red.

Barbara

Katherine glanced at the agenda on her glass. Barbara's version of the two-week agenda contained the slightest information, often just the title for each segment. The first couple of days of the summit concentrated on topics concerning the entire WCA. The end of the first week was focused on the breakout committees. The weekend was filled with social activities and team building. Some paid for by Artemis, some expensed by the attendees or paid for out of pocket. All according to their own governments' regulations. The second week was for the committees to finalize their decisions. The closing session was on Wednesday, but individual committee chairs could extend their agendas through the end of the second week if they chose to do so.

The segments for Katherine's team, highlighted by Barbara in red, had titles like *Brainstorming* with a comment that said, "something new this time." Her team would have to figure out the context and arrange the format for the session. If everything went well, Barbara would get the credit. If it didn't, Katherine would get the blame. She'd dealt with situations like this throughout her career, of course, but it seemed especially grating coming from Barbara. She was the consummate politician, and Katherine had little patience for the way she treated people who did the real work. Yet she would play her role. She knew how important this was to Peter.

Tuesday was more of the same. A bad night's sleep followed by more WCA-related issues and politics. By Wednesday, she was ready to shake things up a little. No 5:45 a.m. alarm. No run. She finally got a decent night's sleep and woke up on her own at 6:30. The extra forty-five minutes were a needed gift. She still got caught up on the news from Suzi over breakfast, one habit that was harder for her to break. Next, she decided not to take the ferry. Instead, she took the elevator down to the parking garage and hopped into her Porsche. She hadn't driven the little convertible in over a month, and it felt great to get behind the wheel. Like most people in a modern metro area, she had no real need to own a car. When you needed to get someplace and didn't want to use public transportation, AutoCabs were generally easier and cheaper. Still, she bought herself this little red Porsche when she was put in charge of Corporate Communications. She liked to drive it to see her parents in Fremont or for the occasional trip up to the wine country.

She pushed the button to drop the top, placed it into gear, and turned the heater all the way up. Silently gliding up the parking ramp and onto the street, she headed for the Bay Bridge entrance. Katherine smiled as she zipped in and out between AutoCabs, just far enough over the speed limit to make it interesting, the spans of the old bridge shooting by overhead. Traffic started to back up in West Oakland at the exit to the Barbara Lee Tunnel, the newest tunnel to Alameda and the most direct way to Artemis. The twenty minutes it took to drive two miles from the exit to the parking garage was a reminder to take the ferry, but she still had a smile on her face as she got out of the car. Driving might be old-fashioned, but it could still be a lot of fun.

The old-fashioned fun continued once she was in the office. Artemis's CMO, Susan Laine, had invited Katherine to sit in on her team's review of the BigNet promo for the Major League Baseball Post-Season. They had done MLB casts in the past from a fan perspective, and that would be available this time as well. However, the big news was the Players Association had finally agreed to have batting helmets fitted with broadcasting coils during the playoffs. It was controversial, but baseball had fallen behind other sports, like American Football, that had long ago included coils on players. Some die-hard fans viewed player casting as damaging to the purity of the sport, but there was no denying baseball was missing out on a major media channel. Artemis had finally pushed Major League Baseball over the top with a revenue-sharing deal that they could not decline. Now Artemis wanted to convince baseball fans that it was a good move, which put the company in the strange situation of using old-world media to promote the casts. This morning, the ad agency brought in a couple of different treatments of everything from billboards to social media vlogs. It was nice to talk about colors, fonts, and images for a change instead of algorithms, brain maps, and the WCA.

As that session wrapped up, she summoned her Porsche to meet her in front of Building 12. It was a warm summer day in the East Bay, and the three-mile drive through the streets of Alameda with the top down was a pleasant one. She parked and walked up to the restaurant. She could see Harbrinder already sitting at a table for two. He stood up as she approached and kissed her on the cheek.

"Hi, beautiful," Harbrinder said. "Thanks for coming."

"Thanks for the invite. It's nice to get off campus for a little bit."

"Yeah, it's been a while since I've been here. The Pho still good?"

"Last time I tried it, yeah."

They sat silently for a moment as they both looked over the menu and tapped in their orders on their glasses.

"So, how's it going," Katherine said to break the silence.

"Yeah, fine, not been sailing much. But I have been thinking about you a bit."

"Oh yeah? Still figuring out how to save me from wasting my life by working?"

"No, I mean, that just came out wrong last weekend, and I wanted to apologize. To be honest, I do have some concerns about Artemis, but that is secondary to how I feel about you. I should have just said that instead of attacking you about the job. I'm sorry."

Katherine stared at Harbrinder for a moment, not quite sure how to take his apology, but knowing that she had to respond.

"Thank you for the apology."

"Again, I am sorry. And you are right, I don't have insight into what it's like and the decisions that need to be made."

"Well, maybe you should take a job at a large company to get a feel for it."

"Maybe I should, but we both know that's not me."

A human waitress brought out their bowls of Pho, two mint lemonades, and some condiments.

"All right, looks good," Harbrinder said.

"Yep, it does," Katherine replied as she thought through her feelings. She showed up, ready for this to be the last time she saw Harbrinder. Chalk it up to another failed relationship and move on. Yet now she wasn't so sure. Harbrinder was a wealthy, handsome, relatively young man who could easily have decided Katherine was not worth the effort. She was sure there were plenty of younger, attractive women who would see him as a real catch. Yet here he was, trying to make it work with her. Maybe she shouldn't be so quick to move on.

"How is your day going so far?" Harbrinder asked between bites.

"Good," Katherine replied. "I reviewed some fun marketing materials this morning. And this lunch gave me an excuse to drive the car."

"Nice day for it."

"Yeah, you bet."

"Did you work on the WCA stuff this week?"

"Oh yeah. Every day from now until the summit. You'd hate it. It's a lot of politics and positioning," Katherine said as she ate her Pho. "In fact, between you and me, the chairwoman is the biggest political hack of them all. She has my team running around like servants while she takes the credit for anything good we do."

"Really?" Harbrinder laughed.

"You bet. Luckily the chair rotates, and she'll be out by next year."

"If the WCA is full of political hacks, why support it?"

"'Full of political hacks' is a stretch. There are politics in any sort of body like the WCA. There are also good people. It's a mixed bag, like anywhere else."

"So, tell me where the good people are. Are they in the Ethics Committee you mentioned? Surely not in Consumption?" Harbrinder said.

"Oh, I guess both have good and not-so-great, like everywhere else."

Harbrinder paused, had a little more Pho, and sipped his lemonade.

"What are the good and the not-so-great parts of the Ethics Committee?"

Katherine stopped eating and looked over at Harbrinder.

"Are we doing this again?"

"No, no, not at all," Harbrinder said. "Look, I honestly want to listen to you and get your insights into that world. We both just agreed I don't know what I'm talking about, but I want to be educated. Really. But we don't need to do it right now. Let's change the subject."

Katherine looked down at her food and remembered that she needed to try.

"I think the biggest issue with the Ethics Committee is the 'committee' part. It is still a bureaucracy. It is slow-moving. The good part is that it's international, and unlike OpenCast, there's still somewhere to go for ethics-based decisions."

"So, they're the ones setting the rules on what can or can't be cast?"

"Only indirectly, and even then it's within the broader WCA. Don't forget there's a Content Committee that handles a lot of that. Ethics is more of a clearing house for complaints."

"I think I remember you telling me once that Ethics was the most powerful committee. Why would you say that if they're just responding to complaints?"

Katherine paused. She did say that months ago. That was a mistake. "Again, I think it is important for people to have somewhere to go with issues."

"But they don't take a more proactive role in casting?" Harbrinder asked.

"Keep in mind I'm not directly involved myself, so I wouldn't really know what happens behind the scenes. I'm just a glorified event planner for the WCA," Katherine responded, her tone starting to become just a bit defensive again.

Harbrinder seemed to read her tone and changed the subject. As they finished their lunch, he made small talk, asking questions about her parents or San Francisco that Katherine responded to briefly in between bites.

"Well, I'll be glad when the whole summit is over," Harbrinder said. "The *Blackfish* misses you, and we need to resume your sailing lessons."

"I can't wait for it to be over either. And yes, sailing would be great. But until then, I need to get back to work. Can I drop you off somewhere?"

"Oh, a ride in the Tanaka speedster! I can't say no to that. Just to the water taxi dock, if you don't mind."

"You got it."

She dropped Harbrinder off with a kiss on the cheek and parked in the garage near Building 12. Then she sat there in her car for a few minutes, feeling more confused than ever. Harbrinder had apologized, hadn't he? Then why was she feeling angry again?

Harbrinder

Harbrinder was still thinking about Katherine as he boarded the water taxi back to Jack London Square. When he had brought up the Ethics Committee, her whole demeanor changed. If their breakfast two weeks ago left him sure Katherine had her doubts about Artemis, this conversation made him confident that *@johnofpatmos* was right. There was something going on with the Ethics Committee. He didn't know if Katherine knew what, but it was clear she suspected something at the very least.

The water taxi docked, and Harbrinder walked over to the *Blackfish*. He opened her up, went down to the galley, and popped open a beer. Returning topside, he sat in the cockpit and thought about what to do next. He'd been trying to take down Artemis for years now, not that they noticed. He was throwing pebbles at a wall and hoping it would collapse someday. He should just move on, but he couldn't let it go. The way they drove their own materialistic agenda at the cost of individual free will made him physically angry. It was all his old hopes for technology twisted into its worst form. Now he had two people on the inside telling him, directly or indirectly, that there was something more going on. Something that Artemis wanted to hide. Maybe something big enough to actually hurt the Goliath.

He needed to find someone who actually knew what was going on with the Ethics Committee. Peter Graham and Linda Ngo must know. Well, good luck getting to them. Same with Frank Kovacs. All untouchable.

Harbrinder took out his glass and went to the WCA website. This year's annual summit in Alameda was on the front page. The kickoff was Monday, July 21st, and it looked like the summit would last two weeks.

He navigated to the Ethics Committee page and saw the thirteen members listed. He searched each of their names and found nothing remarkable. They all appeared to be lifelong bureaucrats.

Harbrinder quietly laughed to himself and took another sip of beer as a crazy idea ran through his mind. He suddenly knew how to find out what was going on. He just needed to ruin his life to do it.

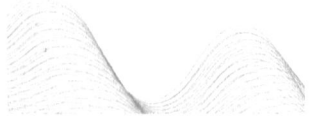

Peter

P eter watched the sun rise over the East Bay hills as he sipped his morning coffee. It was 6:00 a.m., but he was already showered, dressed, and ready to go. It had been years since he was excited for a Monday, but today was the kickoff of the WCA Summit. By the time the summit wrapped up, Peter hoped he would have his life back.

Linda walked into the kitchen wearing her bathrobe and mumbling a good morning as she helped herself to the coffee.

"Morning, sweetheart," Peter said as she sat silently down next to him and took in the view.

Their house sat near the top of the hill on Bluff Point in Tiburon. At fourteen acres, it was one of the largest parcels in Tiburon and the only one that stretched from the top of the hill down to the waterfront. The six-thousand-square-foot main house was relatively modest for the world's wealthiest couple. Without children or an extended family, the bulk of the house consisted of space to entertain and take in the 180-degree views spanning from the Golden Gate to Richmond. Halfway down the road to the dock, there was a separate structure for the human staff. They kept a private secretary, a housecleaner, a handyman, and Jacob, their multi-rotor pilot, on the property. Peter felt separate accommodations were best for everyone. They enjoyed their privacy, and he was sure the staff was happy to have their own retreat as well.

"So, do you think they'll go for it?" Linda asked as the coffee began to work its magic.

"Yep, I do. The United States was the last major piece, and it looks like they're on board. International stability seems to be winning over nationalistic interests for a change. I guess they realized it makes for better business in the long term. By my count, we have a supermajority of the WCA ready to vote in favor. They seem more than happy to take it on and have me out of the picture."

Linda took another sip of coffee and said, "And what about you? Are you really okay with this? I know you keep saying you want to get out of the messy politics of Level 0 embeds, but it's all you've been doing for years now. Are you truly ready to give it all up? Going to take up golf or something?"

"Hell yes, I'm ready to give it up. I also happen to think the WCA is the best vehicle to take it on. It's always been ridiculous for me to be so involved in what gets embedded or not. You know I only ever did it as a hedge against government abuse. Now the various governments can act as a hedge against each other. The thirteen members of the Ethics Committee need a majority vote to recommend an embed. From there, it needs a supermajority of the full WCA to be implemented. I'd be surprised if much gets through at all, and even if it does, we still have the ten-embed limit in place."

"Just seems like with an international body of politicians involved, it's only a matter of time before the Level 0 embeds become public," Linda said. "There's no way they'll keep it a secret."

"Maybe so," Peter responded. "There are a lot of powerful people trying to keep things quiet, but yeah, eventually something will give. Of course, that could happen at any time, with or without me involved. Hell, it already did in Costa Rica. Anyway, better to get out now. Get some freedom while we can."

"Hmmm, maybe. You know people will be looking for a scapegoat though. Might be better to be on the inside when it all goes down."

"Look, if it all goes public, we're fucked. I know that. People will blame us regardless of the good the embeds have brought. They will even forget about the medical advances. They will blame us if I'm on the inside or on the out. Our money and control of Artemis should buy some time. We'll fight in the press, blame the government, and pit the bureaucrats against each other. I know where all the documentation and witnesses are located. And if we're lucky, we'll be able to go live quiet lives in Switzerland or someplace when it's over. If we're not, well, it's been a hell of a ride, Linda."

Linda sipped her coffee and watched the sun play across the water of the Bay.

"I guess it's just as well we never had kids," Linda said.

"I'm sorry I pulled you into all this, Linda."

"I know."

They sat next to each other quietly enjoying the view, the calm, and their coffee until Peter's glass chimed.

"That would be Jacob, letting me know the multi-rotor is ready."

"Well, you better get going. Two more weeks of the ultimate schmoozing, and then hopefully you're done."

Peter got up and bent over Linda to deliver a quick kiss.

"Here's to two more weeks of schmooze," he said as he raised his fist in a mock salute and headed out the door to the pad.

The multi-rotor hangar was located two hundred yards behind the main house. Jacob returned Peter's wave as he approached the vehicle.

"Good morning, Mr. Graham."

"Good morning, Jacob. Nice morning for a flight. Think we can go to the west today?"

"Absolutely."

Tiburon and Alameda were just over eight miles apart as the crow flies. The trip in a multi-rotor took less than five minutes if you were in a hurry. However, Peter was usually willing to add a little time to take the scenic route. He preferred being close to the ground and traveling slowly enough to appreciate the view. Jacob would accommodate by keeping the speed around fifty knots and the elevation just above the five-hundred-foot minimum allowed for multi-rotors. The lower elevation meant you had to go around, instead of simply over, Angel Island, either to the east or to the west. The west took a little longer, but on a clear morning, it provided stunning views of the Golden Gate, Alcatraz, and the light striking San Francisco. Peter took pride in his down-to-earth image, but damn, a commute like this was unashamedly one of his favorite things about being rich.

Jacob circled once over the Artemis campus and gently set the multi-rotor down. Peter jumped out, waved goodbye over his shoulder, and hopped into the waiting company AutoCab.

He was brought to the delivery entrance behind Building 12. No chatting with Sandra today. She would be busy holding court in a packed lobby.

Peter walked purposefully through the back hallways behind the Building 12 conference center. He'd walked these halls many times, preparing for one presentation or another. Just being in the drab space used to get his adrenaline going. Speaking to a large crowd of supporters about something you were sincerely excited about was a particular rush. Now, he felt more like an actor preparing for a performance. Perhaps not even that. Just someone completing a chore. Taking out the trash. Doing the dishes. It was something to get through before the real decisions were made. That was what he was excited about. He would try to channel those feelings if he could.

Peter stepped into the presenter's lounge to find Katherine watching the summit feed on a dedicated screen.

"What's the crowd look like?" Peter asked as he approached Katherine.

"About what we expected. Excluding the Artemis folks and authorized journalists, around 250 people."

A small crowd for a formal production like this. Even smaller when you consider only the eighty voting delegates actually mattered. The rest were just WCA support staff authorized to attend the public proceedings. However, Katherine wasn't holding anything back to make this successful for Peter. The entire conference center was dedicated to the summit.

"Okay, Peter, congratulations for being on time. Now be a good boy and sit over here."

"Ugh, you know I hate this."

"Yes, I do. But we are going to take a little shine off."

Peter sat down in a tall chair as Katherine waved over the makeup artist.

"Just go as light as possible, please," Peter said.

"Of course, Mr. Graham."

"Did you go through the presentation again last night?" Katherine asked.

"Yep, looked good. Be sure to thank the team for me. They did a great job with the visuals."

"I will, and your draft made it easy enough. The theme of 'unity' should play well. You have material for every geo and examples of each committee improving the world by working together. Food redistribution thanks to Consumption, ethnic tensions controlled thanks to Content, hacking prevented thanks to Safety and Security, and public input included thanks to Ethics. You have every reason to be proud of the work, Peter."

Peter knew that she was just trying to get him pumped up for the presentation, which was fine. He did hope the public theme of unity would play well with the delegates who were aware of his private agenda.

Makeup complete and a microphone clipped on, Peter sipped on a glass of water as he watched Barbara Taylor wrap up her presentation.

The stage manager walked into the lounge and asked Peter to come directly backstage to prepare for his introduction.

"With that, I am proud to introduce our keynote speaker, the man who invented casting. Ladies and gentlemen, Peter Graham."

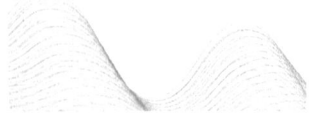

Peter

Tuesday was anticlimactic. It was a full day with the general assembly before the committee work would begin. Peter didn't even have a vote, officially, but he sat through presentation after presentation like a good bureaucrat.

Things began to pick up on Wednesday when the committee meetings started. Peter was there early, drinking coffee and chatting with Michael Sullivan, the Ethics Committee chair, as the other twelve members filed into the breakout room. In addition to Michael representing the European Union, there were representatives from India, the United States, the African Union, Japan, the United Kingdom, Indonesia, Australia, Mexico, Argentina, Canada, Brazil, and Saudi Arabia.

"Anything I should be aware of before we kick off?" Peter asked.

"Oh, I'm guessing you already know where we stand. Probably better than I do. They call them surprises for a reason, but I'm not anticipating any. A few of us may be wondering why you are giving up power. Humans don't normally do that. On the other hand, people usually take power when it's on offer. Fair bet that's the way these folks will vote. But we'll talk about all of that tomorrow morning."

Michael and Peter broke off from each other to greet the other members. It had been the same group of people for a couple of years, and everyone was cordial, if not exactly close.

Jack Price, Katherine's government-assigned employee, approached Michael and then Peter to confirm that the EM shield was active for the room before excusing himself and shutting the door. In a hyper-connected world, the thirteen delegates plus Peter were now isolated. No signals could get in or out of the room.

"Well, everyone," Michael said, "should we get started?"

There was a murmur of assent as the group took their seats. Michael brought out a dense titanium box the size of a deck of cards and placed it on the table. In response, everyone brought out their own glass the size of a tablet and put on a pair of what appeared to be reading glasses. The entire system was called Safety Glass, and it had become the standard for highly confidential communications. The small metal box was a server with no ports, lights, or physical inputs. The server would only connect to a glass that was assigned at the factory or to a dedicated wireless charging and configuration cradle. All data on the box was wrapped in post-quantum encryption. The electronics within the box were only stable in a vacuum. If the metal case was ever broken, the electronics would instantly corrode. The wireless connection protocol itself was both short-range and proprietary. All communications were nonetheless encrypted.

To prevent screen captures, the tablets were unreadable without the dedicated reading glasses. The tablet and the reading glasses had a unique shared secret. The reading glasses were commissioned by the designated user with a built-in retina scan. No one else could use your glasses, and the glasses would only activate when worn close enough for the retina scan. Without the glasses, the display would appear as a shifting, semi-polarized, digital scramble. Seen through reading glasses, your dedicated glass, and only yours, looked perfectly normal. Tampering of any kind, even the shock from dropping them accidentally, would disable the tablet and glasses. No data was stored on the tablets. The records of any motions or votes were recorded on the small Safety

Glass server. In this way, the Ethics Committee could jointly review data and work in complete privacy when they met in person.

The day was spent reviewing the results from the existing Level 0 embeds across geographies. The presentation and the data were formatted by Michael Sullivan, but everyone participated in the smaller setting of the committee. Peter was recognized as the foremost expert in the room, and questions were often sent his way. He didn't mind. It helped pass the time. However, his participation in this committee was one of the things he hoped would change. For now, he played his role.

Measuring the success or failure of a particular embed almost always relied on indirect measures, so the committee tried not to put too much emphasis on minor changes in the behavior of a population. The embeds were set up to be subtle, and changes were usually measured in years rather than weeks or months. That said, looking at those gradual changes was always interesting. For example, "Family is good" was an embed placed in Japan four years ago. The birth rate there had steadily increased every year for the past three years. Mixed in with government incentives, it was hard to say if the embed was the prime factor. Nevertheless, the desired result was being achieved. On the other hand, countries, like America, that have had an embed saying "XYZ country is good" for multiple years were showing a rise in isolationistic nationalism. This wasn't a surprise to Peter. It seemed inevitable from the start. However, Michael bringing it up here was playing to his agenda. Those types of embeds would go away if his proposal went through.

At the end of the day's session, Ren Hayashi, the representative for Japan, approached Peter and asked if he had a moment to talk.

"Of course, Hayashi-san. How are you?"

"I am doing well, thank you. Always a pleasure to participate in this group."

"Yes, I enjoy these smaller gatherings more than the full session."

"Myself as well. I respect all of our colleagues here and yourself as well. That is why I wanted to tell you in advance that I would be voting against your proposal tomorrow. I did not want it to be a surprise."

Peter sighed and looked at Ren. "I have to admit it is not a complete surprise given our past conversations."

"Yes, it is very strange to feel bad for voting against your proposal, which is the same as voting for your continued involvement. Please understand that our government doesn't believe that the standardization you are proposing is in Japan's best interests. Custom embeds, like the one we just reviewed on family, serve the country better than standard global embeds."

"But you will still be able to have custom embeds. Any country can. It just needs to be approved by the larger WCA," Peter said, even though he knew the decision was already made over Ren's head.

"Correct, but will they? It seems like you are opening up embeds to a lot of political intrigue and positioning. Getting a two-thirds vote from the entire WCA would become a full-time lobbying job. As we just mentioned, I much prefer the smaller committee." Ren said with a smile.

Peter didn't have a response for Ren. They both knew the proposal was designed to make custom embeds difficult. Japan would likely lose its ability to use embeds to drive up the birthrate. The world was crowded enough, and it was hard to position Japan's issue as a crisis. Peter doubted they could get a two-thirds majority to approve it. Yet Japan was not alone. Every country would lose its custom embeds. Peter himself would lose "Homosexuality is not a sin" in Uganda. He considered the trade-off worth it. The overall use of Level 0 embeds would drop alongside nationalistic embeds like "America is good." He would no longer have to act as the only foil against governments abusing embeds. If the world, or a single country, felt they had to have an embed, let them make the case and debate it through a formal process.

"Thank you, Hayashi-san, for telling me in advance. I appreciate the integrity of your stance, even if I disagree with the decision."

Ren bowed slightly toward Peter. Peter always messed up this part. He ended up bowing to the same point and then reached out to shake Ren's hand with a smile on his face.

"Now let's go see what kind of dinner they have waiting for us," Peter said cordially as they walked out toward the main hall.

Peter stayed at the group dinner for the necessary amount of time, but no longer, before heading back home in the multi-rotor. He had a good night's sleep next to Linda, and then Thursday morning came. The big day had arrived at last. Again, Peter arrived early. There was no sense in hiding his excitement. Everyone knew where he stood, even if they could not completely understand why. Besides, each of the delegates already knew how they would vote. Like Ren, the decision was already made above their pay grade. Peter could walk in naked, quacking like a duck, and it wouldn't change the voting. In fact, Peter chuckled to himself, if anything, it would help.

Still, there was a protocol to follow. There would be a formal readout and discussion of the proposal. It would allow the delegates to speak on the record, even if that record was restricted to a handful of people.

The committee members filed in, and the mood was casual and light-hearted, just as it had been the day before. After coffee and small talk, Michael Sullivan brought out the Safety Glass server and called the meeting to order.

"If everyone is ready, let's get started. We have a busy day today. This morning, we will review and vote on the proposal to revise how Level 0 embeds are managed. If that proposal is approved, we will have an initial discussion on the first of the new core embeds. Then after lunch, we will take up a discussion on OpenCast."

Michael brought up the full proposal for Level 0 embeds on Safety Glass. It had the simple title of "Proposal 24."

"Let's begin. As a reminder, today's first segment is a formal vote. As such, I'll be recording audio and all text responses onto the Safety Glass server until the voting is concluded. I'm going to assume everyone is familiar with the proposal and has a position on it. So for the record, let me just summarize the major points," Michael said. "Peter or anyone else, feel free to comment if you think I'm missing something critical.

"If adopted, the core Level 0 embeds on a global basis will be recommended by this committee and require a two-thirds vote of the full WCA to be approved.

"All countries within the WCA will have a choice of receiving the same core Level 0 embeds or, alternatively, not receiving any embeds at all. A country may not pick and choose between core embeds.

"A country may petition for a custom embed through this committee. Approval will require a two-thirds vote of the full WCA. No country can have more than one custom embed at a time.

"All current Level 0 embeds will be phased out within a year of the approval of this proposal unless an existing embed is explicitly approved for continuation by the WCA.

"The WCA can approve any additional Level 0 embeds to be phased in as the original ones are phased out.

"The total number of Level 0 embeds shall not exceed ten. This would take the form of a maximum of nine common embeds plus the potential for one custom embed per country.

"Implementation of these policies will be conducted by Artemis.

"Artemis shall assign a full-time liaison to this committee.

"That concludes my summary. Does anyone have any other major points they want to add?"

There was silence and head shaking from the group.

"Okay then, let's open it up for discussion."

More silence. Not that unusual during a formal vote. The recording tended to put a damper on the conversation. Eventually, Charlie Baker, the representative from the United Kingdom broke the ice. "Peter, do you have someone in mind to be the liaison from Artemis?"

"Yes, John Kapoor currently runs Level 1 security for our products. He has been with the company for several years and can be trusted with this kind of data. We haven't approached him yet, of course, but Adam's people have already done the appropriate background checks," Peter replied while nodding toward the United States representative, Adam Perez.

"Why not someone from the current Level 0 team?" Charlie asked.

"Besides me, they're all engineers. John Kapoor has the people skills necessary to interact at this level."

Charlie nodded, and the room slipped back into silence. It seemed that everyone had their minds made up, or at least had their orders from above. Might as well get on with the vote. Then Ibrahim Mansour, the representative from Saudi Arabia, spoke up.

"Okay, if no one else will ask it, I will. Why? Why are you doing this, Peter? Why give up your ability to influence Level 0 embeds given how important they are to the world?"

Peter sighed and then said, "There are practical reasons. Having one person at the hub of these decisions isn't sustainable. What if something happened to me? What if I simply decided to start pushing a particular agenda? Then there's the complexity of implementing different standards across geographies as casting continues to grow. Each embed becomes more and more difficult to implement. So, you can look at this strictly from that level and consider that something has to change. However, on a personal level, I simply want nothing more to do with embeds. The whole concept is distasteful to me. Always has been. When we developed casting, we never wanted Level 2 or Level 0 embeds. There were reasons they came about, but it was never my intent. My dream was to use casting to bring the world closer together, not to manipulate whole populations."

"Now, there are some good things that have come out of Level 0 embeds, and maybe even Level 2 embeds," Peter continued, "and some things that are questionable at best. But regardless, I no longer want any part of it. Casting has matured to the point where there should be a rational process for these decisions, and that process shouldn't depend on one person. I hope that is what happens here. I hope we can implement this proposal and agree on common ideals for embeds. If we can do that, it is at least a step towards my original intent of connecting people instead of controlling them."

The room fell silent again. Michael Sullivan let the silence linger for a few moments before saying, "Well then, should we vote?"

The motion came up on each delegate's Safety Glass. It only took a few moments for the results to come in.

"Looks like everyone has voted," Michael said. "I will now close the voting." Michael paused and then continued, "The proposal to change the management of Level 0 embeds has passed on a vote of 11-2, with Japan and Saudi Arabia voting against. With that, I am stopping the recording."

Peter looked down at the table and smiled to himself. It still had to go before the full WCA in a closed-door session tomorrow, but the voting in the committee felt like it validated his projections.

"Well then, Peter," Michael said with a smile, "I guess we can't kick you out quite yet, but it feels like your days with us are numbered."

"Maybe I'll host a going away party in a year just for us when everything is implemented," Peter responded.

"Sounds grand. In the meantime, let's continue to use you as the cheap resource that you are and get your thoughts on the first set of Level 0 embeds under the new plan. Is everyone ready to move on to the next agenda item?"

The discussion that followed was just what Peter had hoped. Everyone was very engaged, and it became obvious that it would be difficult to get embeds out of committee—which meant it would be even harder to get them through the full WCA. The only existing embeds that had clear support were the first two—"Helping each other is good" and "Theft is bad." Everything else was in question. "Racism is bad" had a chance but seemed a vote or two short. Even "Work is good" did not have the immediate votes. The idea of brand-new embeds was brought up but seemed to go nowhere.

Still, this was just the initial discussion on the topic. Given the WCA approved the changes to Level 0 embed management tomorrow, they would have a full year to get it done. Michael allowed the discussion to continue through lunch before interjecting just before 1:00 p.m.

"Okay, everyone, good talk, but we will have to bring this segment to a close. We have a guest speaker coming in for the next segment on OpenCast. After she concludes her presentation, she will be asked to leave so we can discuss any next steps privately. Peter, would you like to tell Ms. Tanaka she can come in?"

Peter stood up, went to the door, leaned out, and said, "You're up."

As Katherine walked in, Peter continued, "I think you will all remember Katherine Tanaka. She has presented before the committee in the past."

The delegates nodded as Katherine walked in and sat next to Michael.

"Thank you all for having me, and it's a pleasure to speak before the committee again," Katherine began. "I'll be sharing this presentation over my standard glass, which is now sending out a near-field sharing invite. I'll also share it to the in-room screen. This material is considered Artemis confidential, but no restrictions beyond that.

"I'm here to provide a voice to those that can't be heard," Katherine began. "There is a growing segment of the global population that is exposed to the abuse of an unregulated and demonstrably dangerous platform called OpenCast."

Damn, she really is going for it, thought Peter. Well, he'd never known Katherine to do anything half-assed. *So be it.*

Katherine gave a brief overview of the open and poorly controlled nature of the OpenNet. Untrustworthy or deliberately misleading metatags. Homemade coils. Lax geographical boundaries. Then she spent the majority of the presentation sharing the stories of the victims of OpenCast. Men, women, and children raped while casting from both the victims' and criminals' points of view. Casual OpenCast users stumbling onto torture sessions and being traumatized for life. With a brief glance toward the Saudi delegate, she told of heterosexual young men being misled into homosexual casts. Brain damage from a faulty piece of hardware on homemade coils. There weren't a lot of stories, but they were all both true and disturbing.

Of course, in a potentially unsecured presentation like this, she never touched on the fact that OpenCast users avoided Level 0 embeds. She also never mentioned the very public Level 2 advertising embeds missing from OpenCast. They were all smart enough to see that on their own. Instead, she simply empowered the committee to see themselves as heroes in stopping the spread of OpenCast.

"The terrifying thing, ladies and gentlemen, is that OpenCast use has doubled over the last year, and it may well do it again next year. Allowing the continued viral growth of OpenCast is sanctioning the growth of criminality and abuse. The role of the Ethics Committee is to review complaints from the public, and I hope you will take up the cause of these voiceless victims."

Michael broke the silence that followed. "Thank you, Katherine. You've certainly given us a lot to think about."

"Thank you all for your time. I'll let you get to it. I'll have this presentation sent to each of you for reference when you return home."

Katherine picked up her glass and walked quietly out the door.

Peter and Michael briefly caught each other's eye, and Peter just raised his eyebrows. Neither one of them had expected Katherine to come in so hard. She likely exaggerated the ongoing growth potential of OpenCast. He wasn't aware of any projections saying it could double again next year. The stories of abuse were real enough, but humans were awful throughout the world with or without OpenCast. He didn't really have anything against OpenCast and had a soft spot for the lack of embeds it represented. He was just hoping to use OpenCast as a scary story of what could happen without standardization. A common threat they could overcome fairly by being more efficient. Yet Katherine had made OpenCast an urgent issue instead of a long-term business problem. Still, he didn't want to undermine her after giving her permission to bring it up. He looked around the room and saw her presentation had hit home. He sighed to himself. OpenCast was in trouble.

It was Jennifer Hayden, the Australian delegate sitting in while Barbara Taylor held the WCA chair, who spoke first. "Well, clearly we need to do something about this. It is directly within both the public and private capacity of this committee to address this crisis."

"It seems so, but what would you propose?" said Marcia Costa, the Brazilian delegate.

"Well, I think we've just been given the ability to do something about it," Adam Perez, the US delegate, said. "Peter, can we create an embed that discourages the use of OpenCast?"

"You mean like 'OpenCast is bad.' Sure, I mean, it is technically possible. But I'd like to remind everyone that this committee doesn't have that authority quite yet. It still needs to pass the full WCA, and then there's a one-year period to phase it in."

"I think that is far too long to wait," Charlie Barker from the UK chimed in.

"I agree," Adam said.

Neither Charlie nor Adam were ever this vocal about curtailing the negative side effects of casting. Peter realized that the threat of OpenCast to Level 0 and Level 2 embeds had become clear to those two. It was suddenly about protecting the economy. It was about four percent less people consuming what they were told. Which meant there was no fighting the attack on OpenCast. The best he could do was use it.

"First of all," Peter said, "I hope you will all join me in encouraging the rest of the WCA to adopt the proposal we just passed. It is precisely the ability to react to universal concerns like this that would be best handled both quickly and effectively by a standardized approach. Given the current mishmash of embeds and agreements around the world, there is no way I can roll out something like this globally in less than a year, perhaps not less than two. However, with a standard global approach, I can guarantee this in the first wave of embeds if the WCA so decides.

"In the meantime, what I can do," Peter continued, "is roll it out in one country within six months and use that as a test bed to better inform pushing it globally in the future. The United States is the longest and best-documented environment for embeds. Adam, if you can get me permission to roll it out within the United States using our existing process, I'll do it just like I would any of the other embed requests in the past."

"What about the UK," Charlie said.

"And Japan," Ren put in.

"India is the logical one to go first."

"Saudi Arabia would like it as well."

"And Mexico."

"Australia voiced concern first."

"Okay, folks," Peter said. "Let me cut you off there. Welcome to my world. There is no way I could do this in a year with all the countries in this room, much less globally. We need a standard approach so I can shift resources to implementation instead of dealing with the spiderweb of global regulations and agreements in place today. Again, I will commit to the United States if I get permission. In advance, I will treat it as a test within Uganda since that is standard protocol for Artemis anyway.

If we get the new Level 0 policies through the WCA and they want to address OpenCast via an embed, we will be ready within a year."

The room fell silent again. The sudden alignment behind a new embed was in stark contrast to the discussions over lunch. It reminded Peter of the dangers of recency bias that the new system of governance could fall victim to. Still, that was why it was a lengthy two-step process that included the larger WCA. They still had time to think before actually implementing. On a positive note, Peter was sure he had a team of new lobbyists for the Level 0 proposal in the WCA. He would have to buy Katherine that glass of champagne.

Peter

The regular membership of the World Casting Association convened in a closed-door session on Friday morning. Physical security was tight, and the EM shield was up, but no Safety Glass procedures.

Peter sat in the front row as Barbara Taylor called the session to order. After a brief statement on how pleased she was with the summit so far, she got down to business. The session would conduct a series of votes on proposals from the various committees. The Consumption Committee had the greatest number of proposals to offer, but every committee had at least one. There was no discussion or debate. Each proposal was simply referenced by a number, and the vote was conducted.

Peter listened as various proposals came and went. Some he was familiar with, most he didn't care about. Some had been pending for a year, some were put forward this week. Most passed and a few failed. Regardless, he couldn't vote on any of them and was only allowed to attend as a courtesy. He was waiting for Proposal 24 from the Ethics Committee.

When the vote finally came just before lunch, it seemed to hold no more or less procedural drama than any other proposal. It passed with fifty-eight members voting in favor and twenty-one voting against. Japan still voted against. Saudi Arabia, interestingly, abstained. It seemed that Ibrahim had the power to alter his vote while Ren did not. Regardless, it still passed with a supermajority, which was all that mattered. He was free.

The session concluded. Peter waved to a few people and shook some hands but skipped lunch. A decade of weight had been lifted off of his shoulders, and he wanted to take a break from the bureaucracy and grin-fucking. He knew he would have to show his face again next week and then deal with a year of transition, but the path was now secure. He would gift himself the afternoon to celebrate. First though, he wanted to deliver the news to the Level 0 Artemis engineers. They were entitled to know.

Peter walked quickly and directly to Building 15, where the secure Level 0 lab was located. He tried to project an image of deep thought as he walked between buildings to avoid any Artemis employees interrupting him. It worked, and he was soon behind a couple of layers of physical security in the middle of Building 15.

Henry and the other regional engineers were in the lab. Carlos, who handled much of the Spanish-speaking world, was the first to notice Peter's entrance.

"Look out everyone, the boss is here," Carlos said with a grin as the other engineers looked up from their glasses.

"Hello, Carlos, hello all," Peter said as he looked around the lab. "Is everyone here today?"

"Everyone but Chloe," Carlos replied. "She had a doctor's appointment. Girl stuff."

Peter let the childish reply go. Carlos, like all the Level 0 engineers, was a genius in his way. He just never seemed to be able to grow up.

"Okay, well, I have something I want to share with everyone. Perhaps Marcus or someone can catch her up when you see her."

Peter sat down in one of the lab chairs as everyone gathered around.

"This is related to Level 0 embeds and as such is highly confidential. As you all know, the World Casting Association is meeting here on campus this week. You may also remember that I have been trying to get them to streamline how Level 0 embeds are handled. I have good news about that effort, and I wanted you all to be the first to know."

Peter provided an overview of Proposal 24 and how it would be phased in over the next year. He explained the expanded role of the Ethics Committee. He told them most custom embeds would go away, but there may be some new ones coming if the WCA says so. He explained how the team, including Harpo, would be able to focus more on effectiveness and less on regulatory issues.

"If the WCA will manage embeds, what will you do?" Bhavin asked.

"That's a fair question. Seems like you'll also be the first to hear that I'm retiring. Like, really retiring this time and not the kind of retiring that was announced a few years ago. We still have a year, but yeah, I'm going to give it up."

Peter saw a look of concern across a few faces, including Henry's. He expected that. They took pride in working directly with Peter.

"Oh, can I be the new manager, Peter," Carlos said. "I would be perfect!"

The other engineers groaned, and Peter jumped in before things got out of hand. "No, Carlos, I'm afraid not. You will have a new manager, but it will not be someone from this team. It will be someone senior in the company. I can't say who yet until things are final."

"What will the first embeds be from the WCA?" Henry asked.

"I don't really know," Peter replied. "I will say that the First Two—'Helping each other is good' and 'Theft is bad'—still seem to be popular. Some of the other commonly used existing embeds seem less likely to continue. But who knows? A lot can change in a year."

"For you in particular, Henry," Peter continued, "I have good news. This means we're phasing out 'Homosexuality is not a sin' in Uganda by the end of the year. I know you had some concerns about that one."

"Yes, that is good news. Thank you, Peter," Henry replied.

"And, more good news, Henry. There is a new embed for you to write and get ready for testing in Uganda. It is 'OpenCast is bad.' Pretty interesting one, right? I think the United States will want that one too.

There's even a chance the Ethics Committee will want to deploy it globally next year."

Henry didn't respond. He just stared down at the floor. Peter didn't know what to make of that.

Harbrinder

I t was Saturday morning. Harbrinder completed his walk around the lake, stopped to get a cappuccino, and went back home. Another weekend without Katherine. Not unexpected though. She told him long ago that she would be busy representing Artemis at WCA social events. So, his time was his own once again. He decided he would check in on The Project and then take the *Blackfish* down to Half Moon Bay. It had been a while since he'd gotten outside the Gate, and a little adventure always helped clear his mind. Maybe he would figure out a reasonable way into the workings of the Ethics Committee.

He sat down to the large glass at his desk. The OpenCast dev team had completed their review of the code submitted by *@johnofpatmos* and had found nothing blatantly proprietary about it. They put in the disclaimer that they didn't have access to Artemis source code, of course, but it seemed safe to use. Satisfied but still cautious, Harbrinder recommended releasing to the broader community for review as a possible new major release without making any definitive statements around adoption. Let the code bounce around for a while and see if anything else shakes out.

Harbrinder got up to use the bathroom and brought his handheld glass with him. He had just sat down on the toilet when he saw a message from *@johnofpatmos* pop up.

@johnofpatmos: You need to stop the Ethics Committee. Now.

Here we go again, Harbrinder thought. *Big statements without a lot behind them.*

@hstrue: *Yeah, you mentioned that. I've been trying to get more information. Hard to do.*

@johnofpatmos: *No, not look into. Stop. You need to stop them.*

@hstrue: *From doing what? I can't stop them if I don't know what they're doing. If you are serious, you need to stop being vague.*

Nothing for almost a minute.

@johnofpatmos: *They're coming after OpenCast.*

Harbrinder's bowels released.

@hstrue: *What do you mean? Why would they do that?*

@johnofpatmos: *I don't know why. I know that they are.*

Harbrinder was surprised that anyone would bother going after OpenCast. They had been growing pretty well over the last year or so but were still small. It appeared that Goliath had finally noticed David's stones.

@hstrue: *To be clear, you're saying the Ethics Committee is going after OpenCast? How? What can they do?*

Another long pause. Harbrinder washed up and went back to his desk.

@johnofpatmos: *They tell Artemis what to do. They're telling Artemis to make people think OpenCast is bad through embeds.*

@hstrue: *Embeds? That's crazy. Everyone could tell if they did that. It'd be like advertising. Obvious. Would probably get them in trouble with the government.*

No response. Five minutes went by.

@hstrue: *Hello? You need to tell me more.*

@johnofpatmos: *You need to stop the Ethics Committee, or all of your work will be for nothing.*

@hstrue: *Tell me more about how they do it. What proof do you have?*

No response.

@hstrue: *Hello?*

@hstrue: *Hello?*

He looked back over the text thread. *@johnofpatmos* said the Ethics Committee can tell Artemis what to do. Okay, well, yes and they did that publicly. Artemis had agreed to oversight by the WCA a couple of years ago.

Then he said they'd make people think OpenCast is bad through embeds. How could they do that without being obvious? Embeds felt synthetic. Unless Artemis figured out a way to do it without feeling synthetic?

Harbrinder was lost in possibility when his glass chimed again.

@johnofpatmos: This one started in 2035.

@johnofpatmos: 1 file attached

Harbrinder opened the attachment and saw it contained a report on the references in all media to the term "America is good." The report showed the use of that specific term was flat through the early 2030s. In fact, it was used less than both "America is great" and "the United States is good." Then in 2036, "America is good" became the preferred phrase by far, and its use showed multi-digit growth each year.

The report also showed an annual survey run since 2025 that asked Americans if they lived in "the best country in the world." The respondents agreeing with the statement stayed in the mid to low 20th percentile throughout the 2020s, then suddenly dipped into the teens during the Collapse of 2035. However, it started climbing again in 2036 and was currently at a record high of forty-one percent of all Americans agreeing that, yes, they lived in the best country in the world.

Harbrinder felt physically ill as he asked his own AI to run the same report to verify the use of the term "America is good." He placed broad parameters on the search, and it would take several minutes even for his powerful AI to come back with the results. His glass chimed again, knocking him out of his thoughts.

@johnofpatmos: OpenCast is bad.

@johnofpatmos: That embed is next.

@johnofpatmos: You need to stop the Ethics Committee.

Harbrinder didn't respond. He sat at his desk, stunned, angry, and finally accepting what @johnofpatmos said. Yes, they were going after OpenCast, Harbrinder reasoned. It was just starting to grow. They couldn't have that.

Suddenly, the crazy idea he had last week didn't seem so crazy. Yes, it would probably change his life forever, but so what? He was a middle-aged man who had never really accomplished anything significant in his life. This could be the biggest thing since the advent of casting. He had to get to the bottom of it. There was no turning back. No ignoring this.

God, he always knew Artemis was vile. He was right the whole time. He thought it was just the advertising and the consumerism. This went way beyond that. How long had this been going on? What had they been embedding over the years? Political messages? Obedience to the government? Guiding people to make career choices based on what the government wanted? Telling people when or if to have children? It was just like North Korea. No, worse, because it was subtle and hidden. Who knew what decisions people had actually made for themselves over the last eight years?

Harbrinder checked the WCA website. The closing ceremony and dinner were on Wednesday night. He had four days. It was enough time, but he had to get to work.

Katherine

K atherine smiled as Barbara Taylor spoke at the podium. It was the closing ceremony of this year's World Casting Association Summit. The session was open to journalists and support staff. The Building 12 auditorium was full. The summit had gone well. Her team had performed flawlessly. All that was reason enough to smile, but things were about to get even better. Each year's closing ceremony traditionally included the passing of the baton to a new chairperson for the WCA. This was the last time Katherine would have to deal with Barbara. A happy day indeed.

"I'm pleased to announce that the WCA has elected Hien Bui, the representative from Vietnam, to be our next chairperson. I'd like to thank the WCA for this wonderful opportunity and wish Hien all the best in the coming year."

And it was done. Katherine joined the rest of the audience in a standing ovation and started walking to the reception being prepared in the tents outside. Peter came up alongside her and took her by the elbow.

"Well done as usual, Katherine."

"Thank you, Peter. It's easy when you have a good team. But you know all about that, don't you?" she said teasingly.

"Yes, indeed I do."

"Speaking of which," Katherine said, "I believe you owe me a glass of champagne?"

"I do, I do. In fact, I was planning on fulfilling that requirement immediately. If you will follow me?"

Peter led Katherine out to the reception area. There was a large tent, open on three sides, with two bars and a jazz band starting to play. Behind it stood an even larger tent with tables for dinner. The fog enveloped San Francisco across the water as the Island sat in the still-warm air of the East Bay. The delegates hurried to the bar, happy to be released from the conference center. Peter avoided the crowd and brought Katherine to one side of the tent. There, he gestured to someone Katherine couldn't see.

"Peter, what are you doing?"

"One moment, my dear. Ah, here we go."

A pair of human stewards came their way, one carrying an ice bucket with a bottle of champagne and another carrying two glasses.

"Peter . . . what are you doing?"

A steward presented the champagne to Katherine for inspection. It was a bottle of Veuve Clicquot La Grande Dame, an increasingly difficult-to-find champagne. She looked closer at the label. Climate change was gradually destroying the best of French champagne. The vintage was 2030. Still a good year for champagne, yes, but more significantly, the year she had met Peter and joined Artemis.

The bottle itself was not a great expense for the world's richest man. Katherine herself could go through a case or two without denting her bank account. The gesture, however, was priceless. It had been a long time since someone had done something so thoughtful for her. That it would come from Peter, just now, when she knew how important this event was for him, was crushingly sweet. He was her boss, her mentor, and perhaps her truest friend. The disciplined, powerful, and articulate Katherine Tanaka had to catch a tear before it ran down her cheek.

"Thank you, Peter."

"Thank you, Katherine. For the summit, and for everything. Now, before we get too sentimental . . . Gentlemen, if you would?"

The steward opened the champagne, neatly poured two glasses, placed the bottle back into the ice bucket, and stood aside.

"To you, Katherine, La Grande Dame indeed," Peter said, raising his glass.

"To teamwork, Peter," she said, raising her glass in turn.

Peter and Katherine stayed to the side of the tent, but eventually their gravity pulled others toward them. A small crowd gathered, waiting their turn to speak to the famous Peter Graham. Katherine became a sort of waiting room. Delegates would speak to her as they kept glancing over her shoulder to see if they could get to Peter. That was okay. She was used to it. It was part of her job, and she was good at it.

The wine stewards stayed in position. Having two human servants with no responsibilities other than making sure his and Katherine's glasses were full was very unlike Peter Graham. He was clearly celebrating, and Katherine was happy to be a part of it. She would celebrate with him, even as she knew this meant she would see even less of him in the future.

Peter's breaking of convention continued as the dinner bell rang and everyone moved into the larger tent. By her own rules, Katherine had all the Artemis executives distributed out among the tables. Even then, there would be tables without any Artemis employees. There were no personnel to waste. Yet, just as she was about to break away to find her place card, Peter took her by the arm again and led her to a large table. There he had her place card right next to his. On the other side of Peter was Michael Sullivan's name. The other tags she could see were all members of the Ethics Committee. Another faux pas, as committee members were expected to sit next to people outside of their core group during social events. Peter was calling the shots, but there were journalists at this event. She wondered if any of them would make a story of Peter sitting exclusively with the Ethics Committee. Or, God forbid, Peter making such a fuss about Katherine sitting next to him. Would Linda Ngo have to read some trash about Katherine and Peter in the morning? And what about the other Artemis executives? What were they thinking? Would the teacher's pet be beaten up on the playground at recess? Katherine tried to tamp down her professional instincts and enjoy the evening. Peter was clearly beyond caring, and they both knew the honest nature of their relationship. That should be enough.

The wine stewards placed champagne flutes around the table. Then they brought out two more bottles of La Grande Dame and a bottle of dry sparkling cider in deference to Ibrahim. They began filling glasses as the delegates found their place cards and sat down.

Michael Sullivan found his name and looked around the table.

"Is this your doing, Peter? Breaking the rules again, are we?"

"If you would prefer to sit somewhere else, Michael, you may. My preference is that you sit next to me."

"I will if you insist, Peter. But only because I can look past you and see Katherine any time I like," Michael said with a smile.

Once all the delegates were seated, Peter raised his glass to the table and said, "I'd like to propose a toast. To a successful summit and a bright future."

That was all the detail allowed in this semi-public forum, but the delegates raised their glasses and wished Peter the best for the future.

The food started to arrive, and the table broke into individual conversations.

"So, Michael, are you staying on for a few days or heading back to Dublin right away?" Peter asked.

"Heading back early tomorrow morning, I'm afraid," Michael responded. "My youngest has her tenth birthday party on Saturday. Double-digits. I need to get back for it, or my wife will kill me."

"Ah, yes, must keep the wife happy. I don't know much about the kid part, but the keeping-the-wife-happy part I do know a bit about," Peter said with a smile. "Well, by next year's summit, I should be in a position to publicly celebrate. I'm sure we'll have some sort of event out at the house. Would love to have you there."

"That sounds fantastic. Thank you, Peter, and I wouldn't miss it. But, you know, I won't be the Chairman of Ethics at next year's summit."

"Even better," Peter said, still smiling.

After the last course was served, people began to mingle from table to table. Katherine made the rounds with her glass of champagne in hand. She looked back and noticed Peter had stopped drinking. He was standing now, but only to speak to other members of the Ethics Committee. He was keeping a tight orbit this evening, and she had a pretty good guess as to why. He was avoiding being dragged into any lengthy conversations. He probably wanted to go home sober and celebrate properly with Linda.

Katherine looked across the room to see Frank laughing with a member of the Consumption Committee. She sighed. Well, she should probably support her actual boss and find a delegate from that committee to speak to herself. Ah, there was Colette Allard, the French delegate on the Consumption Committee. She looked in need of rescuing from the Chairman of the Safety and Security Committee. An intervention would probably be mutually beneficial.

By the time Katherine had pulled Colette to safety, she noticed that Peter was gone. Good for him and, sadly, good for her. She would stay a bit longer until it was obvious they had left separately. Besides, the champagne was very good.

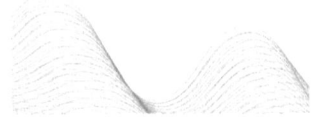

Harbrinder

The idea had occurred to him a couple of weeks ago after his lunch with Katherine. A way to get to the Ethics Committee. He just thought it was a ridiculous, not to mention illegal, thing to do. Now though, they were coming after OpenCast and, by extension, him. They were the ones that had escalated. He had to strike hard or be lost. @johnofpatmos made that clear on Saturday. So he refined his plans and began executing on Sunday. Once he got started, direct action felt just. He had spent years dancing around the edges. Now it was time to take down Big Brother.

Even if successful, it would be a painful loss, emotionally if not financially. He had moved a bit of his liquid US assets to an offshore account. Enough to live on for a year or two, but not so much as to draw attention. He hoped. Anyway, most of his net worth was already overseas in holding companies. He used those companies to help fund The Project, which would soon become more popular than ever if things worked out the way he planned. Yes, he should still be okay financially. Emotionally, it was a lot harder. He had grown up in the Bay Area, and his life was here, such as it was. He was sure his house and, worst of all, the *Blackfish*, would be ripped apart by the government in the coming weeks. Yet it needed to be done. It would be the culmination of his life's work. He would be a hero in the eyes of millions and, if his hunch was right, in Katherine's eyes too.

The first part of the master plan involved picking up four dozen donuts and heading to the Singh Animal Shelter in San Leandro. Harbrinder drove his own car, jumped out with a bag containing half the donuts, and greeted the Sunday group of volunteers with a smile. Sunday was a busy adoption day almost exclusively managed by volunteers. Most of the admins and all the veterinary staff had the day off. The volunteers felt honored to be served donuts by *the* Harbrinder Singh. Harbrinder, for his part, said he just wanted to swing by to thank everyone and transfer some needed medical supplies over to Redwood City. He badged himself into the operating room and put a bottle of ketamine, a bottle of isoflurane, an atomizer, and a small bottle of nitrous oxide into the donut bag. The combination was the standard anesthetic kit for spaying and neutering. Harbrinder walked out smiling and waving to everyone. He then repeated the process in Redwood City, saying he had to bring some medical supplies to San Leandro.

Eventually, what he did would be noticed. However, who was going to call the police on Harbrinder Singh, lover of animals and benefactor to the two largest animal shelters in the Bay Area? At the very least, it would take a couple of days. Then maybe they would justify it by saying he must have forgotten to drop it off. Or maybe: *"Hey, you know those rich guys, they're always looking for new ways to party. And are we really sure it was him? Maybe we missed something?"* Worse case, he was sure even the most uptight, by-the-book vet would call him before calling the authorities. By the time all of that played out, he would either be in China or jail.

By Sunday afternoon, he was in his AutoCab service yard, experimenting with the placement of the isoflurane atomizer and nitrous oxide under the seats of a cab. As the sun set, he had a mounting option and remote trigger he was happy with.

The internet helped him estimate the dosages. He wasn't too concerned with side effects, so he erred on the high side. The ketamine he would only need three, or worse case four times, and he had enough isoflurane to outfit twelve AutoCabs. Twelve should be enough.

The ketamine and the isoflurane were the only controlled substances involved. Everything else was commercially available. Monday morning was spent picking up atomizers, nitrous oxide, some networking gear, wiring harnesses, micro-servers, consumer-grade EM shields, mounting hardware, and ID stickers needed to outfit all the AutoCabs. Then he found a used twenty-five-foot electric tender for sale, gave it a quick inspection, paid full price, and brought it over to a guest slip in the Berkeley Marina. Then back to the AutoCab yard for a long night of installing equipment.

A few hours of sleep and a lot of coffee transitioned him into Tuesday. This would be a day spent on more familiar ground, writing software with the help of his AI.

He had the AutoCabs physically ready. Twelve had the gas installed. A thirteenth AutoCab without anesthetics would act as a decoy. He randomly changed the ID numbers on the side so they no longer tracked back to his fleet. He had them all networked via VPN to mask the online traffic. However, to the AutoCab app, they still appeared as the same cabs owned by his holding company. That would be the next problem to solve.

AutoCab had pretty decent security when it came to preventing people from stealing fares. It was hard to intercept payment. However, AutoCabs came and went from fleets, so APIs were available to switch out the vehicles in bulk. These APIs were set up to make it hard to steal fares, but not for a legitimate account holder to credit fares to another account. Nobody was too concerned with security in that scenario. He copied the IDs of thirteen random AutoCabs. When Harbrinder flipped his virtual switch, his thirteen AutoCabs would show up as belonging to his competitors in the area. A little compensation for their trouble when the police show up.

The next bit of code required was an on-demand transfer of the AutoCab ID from any of his twelve AutoCabs to the thirteenth that would be acting as a decoy. The trick would be doing it instantaneously. All of this would be discovered once an investigator or AI got access to the AutoCab logs. He just needed time before that happened.

The final bit of software for the day was straight out of The Project. There was a little app written by one of the devs that allowed you to clone an Artemis coil to make an OpenCast coil. It was an interesting idea intended to help accelerate the migration to OpenCast. However, it never got much traction because it just wasn't as accurate as using a complete brain scan file, which any user had access to with a HIPAA request. Yet it worked well enough for his purposes. He dusted off his own Artemis coil, got out the required OpenCast hardware, and familiarized himself with the process until he was happy. You had to first connect to an Artemis cast to get the Artemis coil to initialize and begin receiving so you could clone what it was doing. He couldn't figure out a way around that step. However, once you did connect, you could read how the coil was targeting the brain and duplicate that on OpenCast.

Wednesday morning dawned, and now it was down to logistics. Harbrinder brought some supplies to the *Blackfish*. Then he drove over to Berkeley to get his new tender and motored it back to Jack London Square. He tied the tender off to the stern of the *Blackfish* and towed it over to Richardson Bay, dropping anchor in an isolated spot on the edge of the anchorage, just outside the protection of Belvedere Island. He would have to deal with the currents here, but he didn't dare pull further into the anchorage next to the other boats. Once he was satisfied that the anchor could withstand the tide, he locked up the *Blackfish*, left her there, and took the tender back to Berkeley. It was Wednesday afternoon. The closing ceremony of the WCA Summit would be starting soon. He was ready.

Back home, Harbrinder once again went through all his code. He tried, and failed, to get a little sleep. Just before midnight, he convinced himself that a trial run of the AutoCab ID swap would be a good idea. He knew the big closing ceremony would still be going on. He triggered the swap and then assigned the twelve active AutoCabs to the Artemis campus.

As the AutoCabs began to pick up passengers, he monitored the live interior security feed that was standard on all AutoCabs. The destinations of the fares implied they were mostly for Artemis employees going home, which was a good sign. Almost all of the delegates should be staying at the Artemis Hotel, a short walk from Building 12. No reason they wouldn't be staying at the on-campus hotel, but his plan was completely dependent on it.

The ID swap appeared to be working as planned. The fares were being credited to his competitors. As Wednesday night became Thursday morning, Harbrinder was prepared to set the AutoCabs back to standby. Then an AutoCab picked up a passenger he recognized. It was Katherine. Going home. Alone. Harbrinder watched. He couldn't help himself. She was beautiful. She had a small smile on her face. Was she thinking of him? He thought so. He briefly considered activating the isoflurane/nitrous mix to bring her to him. Then he realized how crazy that was and turned off the video feed. He would see Katherine soon enough.

Shaking off the distraction, Harbrinder brought the remaining AutoCabs back to standby and examined the results of his test run. Yes, he was ready. He just couldn't stop worrying. He stayed up the rest of the night checking and double-checking every possible link. It wasn't that he was concerned about getting caught. He knew that would happen. It was just a matter of delaying the inevitable long enough to get what he needed and begin the multi-stage trip to Hong Kong.

Around 5 a.m. on Thursday, he re-activated his AutoCabs and initiated the ID swap, assigning the fleet to the Artemis Hotel. The delegates should start leaving for the airport this morning. He just had to wait for the right one.

He checked the AutoCab app. It was early, but of the nineteen cabs near the hotel, twelve were his. He liked the odds. The majority of AutoCab owners were passive and let AutoCab determine routes to maximize profitability. Hopefully, the algorithm would see the area was saturated and suggest other locations for any additional cabs.

He got his first hit at 6 a.m. The facial recognition on his AI said it was Suijan Bhati, a member of the Consumption Committee. On another day, Harbrinder would have picked him on principal. Luckily for Suijan, Harbrinder had bigger fish to fry, but he smiled at the idea of gassing him anyway. In the end, he let the cab go with instructions to return right away without another fare. It would be back in the queue by 7 a.m.

He lost five more cabs to delegates from Content, Consumption, and Safety and Security. Then at 6:45, he got his first viable target. He didn't need his AI to identify this one. It was Barbara Taylor. The chairperson of the WCA. He was giddy with excitement. Now he knew what attracted people to the hunt. He had bagged the big one. His fingers began dancing on his glass to execute the next phase, and then he paused. Did Barbara Taylor know the details of the Ethics Committee? He thought she probably did. But just probably. Not definitely. Then he considered the attention that came with the chairperson of the WCA. Attention that he didn't need. Attention that might cost him his freedom, and for someone who might not even have what he needed. With a sigh, he decided to let Barbara Taylor go.

Cabs seven and eight were also lost to insignificant delegates. Now cab number one had returned to the queue. A queue fourteen AutoCabs long. Harbrinder currently had four out of the fourteen cabs in line. His odds were getting worse. He realized what was happening. Artemis employees were coming to work, drawing more and more AutoCabs to the area. The AutoCab algorithm must have determined that these cabs were better off getting in line here than fighting traffic for another fare.

Ten minutes later, Harbrinder's luck started to turn. In cab number nine, the AI showed Ibrahim Mansour, an Ethics Committee member from Saudi Arabia. He would do. The cab pulled away from the hotel as Harbrinder once again prepared his tools. Then he glanced over as cab number ten picked up its fare. To his delight, it was another delegate that he recognized. On his screen was the wooly face of Michael Sullivan, Chairman of the Ethics Committee.

Okay, Ibrahim, Harbrinder thought as he shifted his attention to cab number ten. *This is your lucky day. Why take a little fish when you can hook the chairman?* Michael Sullivan would be the target. He was guaranteed to have all the information Harbrinder needed while still being relatively obscure.

No more second thoughts. Nitrous oxide started streaming across the isoflurane atomizer as the cab headed toward the Oakland Airport. It would take at least fifteen minutes for the anesthesia to take hold. The gas had to fill the cab, and Michael Sullivan was not a small man. Traffic on the way into Artemis was slow, but the outbound traffic was moving much too quickly for Harbrinder's liking. He needed more time. He manually rerouted the cab down Central Ave and away from the Posey Tube. It would add another ten minutes to the trip, which should be enough. He watched as Michael glanced about and then went back to staring at his glass. No visible signs of concern.

As the cab approached Webster St., Harbrinder sent it back on track for the Posey Tube. He watched with building excitement as Michael yawned and looked down at his glass. Was it working, or was he just tired? He couldn't see if Michael's eyes were shut. It didn't matter. He had to keep to his plan. Once the cab was midway through the tube, Harbrinder activated the EM shield and locked all the doors. Only his signal would get in or out now. If Michael was awake enough to notice, there was no longer anything he could do to stop it. A few minutes passed, and the cab made the turn down 7th St. Harbrinder watched with satisfaction as the glass fell out of Michael's hand onto the floor. He was out.

Three minutes later, Harbrinder had the cab heading down Madison Street, apparently still on route to the Oakland Airport. Madison Street passed under the 880 freeway, covering it from above. It was here that Harbrinder had decoy cab number thirteen waiting. As Michael's cab approached, Harbrinder initiated the ID swap between the two cabs. He then sent cab thirteen on its way to the Oakland Airport while Michael's cab pulled into the now-empty parking space under the freeway.

At home, Harbrinder ran his staged scripts, deleting all locally stored information. Almost everything, including his AI, was in a cloud environment managed by one of his holding companies. Still, he didn't want to leave any pointers. Next, he grabbed a stuffed backpack and walked out his front door. He turned to give his house one last look and jumped on a bicycle for the downhill ride to the cab waiting for him on Madison Street.

Five minutes more and he was a block away. He got off the bike, left it behind for good, and brought out his glass as he walked toward the cab. He tapped in a few commands to turn off the nitrous, lower the windows, and activate the fan. As he approached, he looked inside and confirmed that Michael was still passed out. Harbrinder stood there, casually checking his glass while leaning against the cab. He allowed the stream of traffic to pass by and renew again as the cab continued to vent. A couple of minutes later, he opened the back door and sat down next to Michael, who had just begun to stir. Still using its false ID, Harbrinder directed the AutoCab to go to the DoubleTree Hotel at the Berkeley Marina and look for fares. As soon as they started to move, Harbrinder brought out a syringe of ketamine and injected it into Michael's arm. Michael slumped back into his seat.

Harbrinder went through Michael's pockets and checked his body for any electronics. There was just Michael's one glass on the floor, which Harbrinder turned off and placed in his own pocket. Then he opened

up the backpack and brought out a large sail bag. It was designed to hold
the mainsail of a small sailboat. Yet if it wasn't for the colors and logos,
it would look like a body bag, which was how Harbrinder intended to
use it.

He reached over and unfastened Michael's seatbelt as the AutoCab
worked its way to Berkeley. He grabbed Michael's feet, placed them
in the sail bag, and roughly pulled him onto his side. Trying to get
Michael's large frame into the sail bag within the tight confines of the
AutoCab made him doubt his choices this morning. Ibrahim was a
smaller man. The way he had to climb over, wrestle with, and generally
manhandle Michael to get him into the bag would have been comical
in a different context. As it was, Harbrinder was simply grateful to have
gotten it done before the cab pulled up at the DoubleTree Hotel.

Instead of picking up fares, he took the AutoCab out of service and
directed it to a nearby parking lot. Harbrinder then walked down to
F Dock next to the DoubleTree. There he grabbed one of the dock
carts behind the gate and went back to the cab. He took all of Michael's
luggage, threw it into the cart, and wheeled it down to the tender.
Returning again, he positioned the cart next to the cab's door and
unceremoniously plopped Michael into it. He planned on this maneuver
looking like nothing more than the loading of a heavy mainsail, but the
whole thing now seemed ridiculous. He wouldn't be fooling anyone
paying close attention. Michael was just too large. Luckily no one was
nearby, and anyway, there was no other choice but to keep moving.

Harbrinder rolled the cart through the gate and down to his electric
tender docked below. He secured the cart in place before grabbing the
sail bag and heaving it part-way on board. Maneuvering to the other
side, he flipped the rest of the mass forward and onto the deck with a
thud.

He found himself sweating profusely and needed to catch his breath.
The lack of sleep, physical effort, and stress were catching up with him.
Breathing deeply alongside the tender, he suddenly leaned over the sail

bag and unzipped it over Michael's face. A little pasty-looking, but still alive.

Releasing the dock lines and jumping on board, Harbrinder maneuvered the tender out of the marina and motored over to the *Blackfish* at speed. The cool morning air dried his sweat and calmed him down again. He reached for his glass and instructed all thirteen AutoCabs to go into standby mode at random locations after their next fare.

Glancing down at the sail bag on deck, Harbrinder realized he had done it. He had the Chairman of the Ethics Committee at his feet. He thought back on the last few hours and tried to analyze where he would get caught. Probably in the AutoCab logs, but even those would just point to a holding company. How long did he have before his name came up directly? Forty-eight hours? Less? The thought interrupted his feelings of triumph as he approached the *Blackfish*.

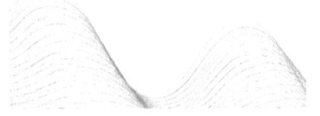

Katherine

The alarm clock went off at 5:45 a.m. As usual, Katherine was already awake. It was a Friday, but she still wanted to get back to her routine. After the marathon of the WCA Summit, she had spent Thursday recovering. She had slept in, worked from home, and generally got caught up on all the work that wasn't the WCA. Now she was ready for things to get back to normal. A run, breakfast, and the ferry ride into the office.

She put on her running clothes and checked her glass before heading to the elevator. Then she stopped and sat down. Michael Sullivan was reported missing. Felix Bauer, the EU liaison on her Government Affairs team, had sent her a report with what little information they had. Michael had gotten into an AutoCab yesterday morning at the hotel, presumably heading to the airport. He was booked on a flight home two hours later. He had never boarded the plane. Never went through security. There was no record of anyone fitting his description exiting an AutoCab at the airport. The last known location of his glass was under the estuary in the Posey Tube. The service hadn't been pinged since then. Strangely, the only other sign of him was his coil briefly connecting, but the location was masked by a VPN tunnel.

She checked for more information. Nothing. If this was a normal missing person, she wouldn't expect much more. It hadn't even been twenty-four hours. However, this was the Chairman of the Ethics Committee, and she knew there would be multiple federal agencies quietly on top of this already. She sent messages to the US government liaison on her team, the head of Artemis physical security, and, with gritted teeth, to Jack Price. She resented Jack keeping an eye on her for the government but also knew he had direct ties to the intelligence community. She asked all of them to keep her in the loop if there was any more information. Finally, she sent a message to Peter and Frank to make sure they were aware.

Katherine just sat there looking out her window for a few minutes. It was very out of character for Michael to just disappear like this. Something must have happened. Whatever it was, it seemed intentional. Was it possible that Michael ran away with information about the Ethics Committee? No, she knew Michael well enough to know he wouldn't do that. Not just out of duty, but because he would never leave his family behind. Oh wow, his family. Katherine sent another message to Felix Bauer asking if the family had been informed and, when appropriate, to let them know Artemis would do everything it could to support the search.

Then Katherine pinged Suzi, the department AI, and made news about Michael Sullivan her top priority. Any additional information was to trigger an alert on her glass. She stared down at her running shoes. Katherine decided it would be best to keep to her routine and head into the office after her run. However, she would break her own rule and keep her glass with her for the run just in case.

Katherine arrived at Artemis headquarters without any updates on Michael. There had been replies to her emails expressing concern, including from Peter, but nothing substantial. Walking to her office, she saw Jack Price standing there waiting for her.

"Hello, Katherine, do you have a minute?"

"For you, Jack, just at the moment, I do," she said as she opened her door and let him in. Jack entered and shut the door behind him.

Katherine remained standing as she asked Jack if there was any news.

"Nothing to report on my side, but I was wondering if I could ask you a few questions?"

Katherine stared at Jack as she realized she was about to be interrogated by her junior employee. A junior employee who, among other things, wouldn't hesitate to report her to the Feds if he thought she was a problem. She briefly considered telling him to fuck off, but that wouldn't help bring Michael back. She decided to let Jack ask his questions while making it abundantly clear that he would be paying for it in menial tasks as soon as this was resolved.

"Take a seat, Jack." Katherine took her own chair behind the desk.

"Thank you."

They stared at each other silently for a moment until, finally, Katherine said, "Go ahead."

"You were one of the last people to see Michael. You, Michael, and Peter Graham all sat next to each other at the closing dinner. By your own rules, that was a break of protocol. Can I ask why the break in protocol and what was discussed?"

The little fucking shit. "There were two reasons for the break in protocol. First, Peter wanted to thank me for a successful summit. Second, he wanted to thank the Ethics Committee for their work during the summit."

"So the change in protocol was initiated by Peter Graham?"

Katherine stared at Jack for a moment. The fucked up little fucking shit. "It was."

"And was the work of the Ethics Committee discussed?"

"It was not."

"What was discussed?"

"I primarily remember Michael looking forward to his daughter's birthday this weekend. Peter and Michael also discussed seeing each other again next year."

"What else?"

"Michael complimented the catering on the chicken cutlet."

"That's it?"

"Pretty much. As soon as the last course was served, I started visiting other tables. Per protocol."

Jack stared at Katherine for a moment.

"Was there anything unusual about Michael's behavior?"

"Not at all."

"Okay, Katherine. Thank you for taking my questions."

"Whatever helps resolve the situation."

Jack got up to leave. As soon as the door was open and anyone outside might hear, Katherine said cheerfully, "Oh, and Jack? If you would be a dear and get me a cappuccino when you have a moment?"

Jack turned, met her eyes, smiled, and walked off.

The rest of the day was spent, unsuccessfully, trying not to worry about Michael. There was a personal angle to this; Katherine truly liked Michael, but there was also the professional impact. Whatever happened, there would be some fallout from this. Best case, it was a random incident. Worst case? This was a targeted attack against a member of the WCA. Specifically a member of the Ethics Committee. Why would someone do that? What was their agenda? Did they know what the Ethics Committee really did? Would this become public, and if so, how would Katherine spin it?

By late afternoon, there was still no news. Katherine sat in her office, staring out at the Bay. She had thought through all the angles. Reached out to the proper people. Now she was just spinning her wheels. She needed to take her mind off of it for a bit. She watched the sailboats go by and thought it was just as well that she was seeing Harbrinder tonight.

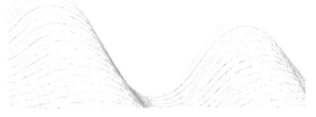

Harbrinder & Michael

When he first pulled up to the *Blackfish* with Michael stuffed in a sail bag, he was unsure if his nerves would hold up. Despite being a sociopath, Harbrinder had never intentionally physically hurt someone. He expected torturing someone might be taxing, or worse, unleash something evil inside him. He told himself to think of it as a medical procedure or to focus on the billions of people being impacted by Artemis. Yet none of that was really necessary once he got started. The emotional detachment his dad was concerned about was an asset for this work. If anything, his main reaction was disgust, but not with what he was doing. No, he was disgusted by Michael. He expected to be dealing with a noble opponent, the Chairman of the dreaded Ethics Committee. Holding out against anything Harbrinder sent his way. Instead, he got a blubbering mass that wet himself and cried to go home.

The process itself was straightforward. He had dragged Michael, still in the sail bag, down the companionway into the *Blackfish*. Once inside, he stripped him naked and propped him up on the metal and plastic chair he had secured to the mast. It was one of those toilet chairs you see in hospitals or elderly homes. The seat was an open ring with a bucket beneath. Harbrinder wanted to keep the cleanup simple when Michael started shitting and pissing himself.

After making sure he was tied securely in place, Harbrinder went through Michael's luggage. He quickly found what he was looking for. Michael's Artemis coil. He had counted on it being there. After all, who wouldn't bring their coil to a casting conference? Then, an unexpected bonus in the carry-on bag. A Safety Glass server with viewing glasses. Harbrinder knew he couldn't personally decrypt a Safety Glass server, but he would bring it with him to Hong Kong. With time and the proper equipment, he bet someone in China could pull information from the server.

Harbrinder brought out his OpenCast equipment and double-checked that the EM shield and VPN tunnel were configured correctly. He then secured the required sensors to Michael's coil. Harbrinder placed the coil onto Michael's head as he started to stir and powered the coil on. He watched the readout as it initialized. It was working. A few moments later, the OpenCast app showed the clone was complete. Harbrinder removed and powered off Michael's coil.

As Michael continued to stir, Harbrinder decided to tie a blindfold in place but left him ungagged. He wanted him to be able to answer his questions, and besides, no one would hear him scream out here.

"Michael, can you hear me?" Harbrinder ventured.

No response.

He tried again a few minutes later. "Michael, I need you to listen to me. It is important for your personal well-being that you listen to me now."

"Hmmm, wait, uh, I can't see. Why am I tied up? Where the hell am I?" Michael said.

"You are in a safe place for now. If you want to stay in this safe place, I need you to answer my questions."

"Who are you? What the hell is going on?"

"I'm a friend of humanity. You need to answer my questions."

"I don't know who the fuck you think you are, but you are in a shit load of trouble."

"I am not the one in trouble at the moment, Michael. Now, tell me about the Ethics Committee."

It went back and forth like this between Harbrinder and Michael. Each threatening the other. Neither giving useful answers. Eventually, Harbrinder sighed, got up, and strapped the newly cloned OpenCast coil onto Michael's head.

"What the fuck is that?" Michael said.

"It's an OpenCast coil, Michael, I thought it was time for you to get a look at the competition. I'm just going to let it run for a few hours, and then we can talk again."

Harbrinder turned on the coil and ran the scripts he had prepared. He had always known about the dark parts of the OpenNet. The places where his cousins, the psychopaths, ran free. These spaces were the price of freedom and deregulation. Like any sane man, he avoided them and actively supported tools that allowed the average OpenCast user to do the same. But he knew where they were. He knew the meta-language of these purveyors on the edge of humanity. So he simply wrote a script that would bounce between dark casts and funnel whatever was there into Michael's reality. Other than preventing cardiac arrest, there were no fail-safes, no way for Michael to turn it off. He didn't know exactly what Michael would experience. He had no desire to try it out for himself. However, he was confident that over the next few hours, Michael would be tortured in multiple different ways, raped repeatedly, and humiliated beyond his imagination. So he just let the script run.

He had to put a gag in Michael's mouth within the first five minutes. Not that anybody was going to hear, but the screaming made it hard for Harbrinder to relax. Even with the gag in place, the whimpering continued. Harbrinder put in noise-canceling earbuds. After watching for a few more minutes, he decided to take his glass with him into the rear cabin. He checked the news feeds. No mention of Michael. Harbrinder closed his eyes and checked his own mental state. He knew he was supposed to be feeling bad for Michael, but he didn't. The feeling just wouldn't come. He felt . . . something . . . but it wasn't bad. After all, this was necessary to defend right from wrong. It was more important than Michael. Harbrinder took a nap.

Two hours later, it was the smell that woke him up. Harbrinder dry-heaved as he opened the cabin door. Michael was pale, collapsed against the straps of his chair, his legs splatted with excrement, and the bucket was surprisingly full.

Harbrinder turned on the cabin fans and opened a hatch. Then he paused the script on the OpenCast coil. Michael moaned as Harbrinder removed the gag.

"Michael? Michael, are you ready to answer my questions?"

"Why? Why would anyone do this?"

"Oh, not quite yet? Okay, let's let it run a little longer."

"No!"

But Harbrinder had started the script. Michael cried out. Harbrinder, still retching at the filth, carried the full bucket up the companionway to dump it over the side. He put a spare bucket in place just in case as he continued to clean up. Eventually, he went back up the steps with the last load of muck to throw overboard. Pausing in the cockpit, Harbrinder couldn't help but notice how beautiful it was at night in the anchorage. He sat for a moment, ignoring Michael's sobs down below. He could see the city lights glistening against the water, look up and see the stars, or glance over at a peaceful evening in Sausalito. He would miss this place.

After coming back down, he stopped the script again. Before Harbrinder could say anything, Michael moaned, "I'll tell you. I'll tell you whatever you want to know."

And Michael did tell Harbrinder. He told him about the Level 0 embeds. He told him they had been in place since the very beginning. He told him about the different embeds in different countries, but that now there was an effort to standardize them. He confirmed that they were going after OpenCast next.

A range of different feelings ran through Harbrinder. Surprise at how deep it went, anger at the manipulation, but above all, the emotion that stood out was validation. He had been fucking right all along. He knew it. Artemis was the enemy of humanity. They were manipulating most of the planet and had been doing it for almost a decade. "Capitalism is good." "Work is good." "Theft is bad." "America is good." Creating a population of obedient sheep consuming what they were told. Harbrinder Singh was fucking right!

He looked back over at Michael and smiled. "Okay, Michael, that's very good. Isn't it great to tell the truth? Now, it's been a big day for both of us. You wouldn't know this, but it's very late at night. I think it would be best if we tried to get some sleep, don't you? If you continue to cooperate, this should all be over by tomorrow."

Harbrinder grabbed a beer from the ice box and quickly drank half of it. He stared over at Michael for a moment, opened another beer, and poured some into Michael's mouth.

"A little celebration."

"Please let me go."

Harbrinder rolled his eyes, put the gag back in place, and went to the rear cabin to finish his beer and ping Katherine. Then it was back to the noise-canceling earbuds and the sleep of the righteous.

On Friday morning, Harbrinder had an energy drink and a protein bar for breakfast while enjoying the view from the cockpit of the *Blackfish*. Going back down below, he noticed Michael was awake, so he removed the gag and put some water into his mouth.

"Please let me go. Please," Michael said again.

"Not quite yet, Michael. I have something I need to work on, and then I will need your help again. Here, let me give you something to do. This cast is a popular one that's just coming online. The guy is great. He should be starting the prep for the lunch rush."

Harbrinder brought up the ramen chef in New York City as Michael let out another whimper.

"Now now, Michael. The worst thing that's going to happen here is an argument with the sous chef. No more bad casts as long as you cooperate."

That settled, Harbrinder took the brain map from the Artemis clone and began working on an OpenCast broadcasting coil for Michael.

A couple of hours later, Harbrinder took the receiving OpenCast coil off of Michael's head and replaced it with the larger broadcasting coil. He removed the gag and gave Michael some more water. Then he took a wet rag and cleaned up Michael's face the best he could.

"What's that on my head?" Michael asked nervously.

"That is a broadcasting coil that I made just for you. But don't worry, I'm not going to be broadcasting you out on the OpenNet. What I am going to do is use it to monitor your reactions to everything you say." It was an accepted use of broadcasting coils in legal proceedings, albeit usually using Artemis coils. A broadcasting coil conveyed a person's physical reactions by relaying signals from the hypothalamus. If you captured those signals in reaction to statements, it could be used as a very accurate lie detector.

"Now," Harbrinder continued, "I'm going to walk you through those questions from last night again. I want you to answer truthfully. If it looks like you're lying, it's back to the dark casts, understood?"

"I haven't lied! I won't lie!"

"Okay, that's good to hear. Let's get started."

Harbrinder set up a small glass next to Michael's face. It displayed the relevant readout from Michael's broadcasting coil. He then began a conventional video recording, framed to show Michael's face and the coil readout. Finally, he turned on a recording of the broadcasting coil to retain it as a separate archive. He digitally watermarked both files as they recorded. Between the two files, he would have all the proof he needed to bring down Artemis.

Michael answered all of Harbrinder's questions, truthfully and without hesitation. It was all documented and digitally secured.

That done, Harbrinder checked his watch. It was almost time to go. With no preamble, Harbrinder stuck Michael with a ketamine injection. Once he was out, he cleaned him up, put his clothes back on, and strapped him down to a bunk amidship. Then he tucked him in with a blanket, covering the straps. To anyone coming aboard, he would look like a man peacefully sleeping on a sailboat.

Harbrinder carried the metal and plastic hospital chair up to the cockpit and threw it overboard. He put another ketamine syringe in his pocket, locked up the *Blackfish*, hopped in the tender, and powered across the Slot on his way to pick up Katherine. Behind the wheel, gliding atop the water at speed, he was proud of himself. He had done what was needed. Now he hoped he had enough time left to get what he wanted.

Katherine & Harbrinder

K atherine took the four o'clock ferry back to San Francisco, still thinking about Michael but knowing there was nothing more she could do. Harbrinder said he would pick her up at 5:30 for an evening sail. He said that he had something special to show her. God, she hoped he wasn't going to propose or something similarly horrible. Years ago, she had a relationship that was starting to come apart, and the poor guy proposed out of desperation. Embarrassing. She was close to a similar collapse with Harbrinder, but he still seemed to be trying, so she decided to as well. At least for now.

She changed into warm activewear and walked down to Pier 1 1/2, arriving exactly on time. At first, she thought Harbrinder was late, which would be no real surprise. It was a small dock, and the *Blackfish* was nowhere to be seen. However, as she drew closer, she saw Harbrinder waving to her from one of those electric tenders with the rigid inflatable sides seen around big yachts.

"What do we have here?" she said hopefully as she got closer. "Is this what you wanted to show me?"

"This is a new toy, but no, I have something better to show you on the *Blackfish*. This will get us there in a hurry if you'll step aboard, my dear."

"Looks fun!" Katherine said as she climbed onto the tender and sat behind him.

Harbrinder turned them around and headed along the city front at thirty knots.

"Woohoo! This is a bit faster than the *Blackfish*. Does she have a name?"

"No name. Not going to have her long enough for a name," Harbrinder shouted back over the wind.

"Why wouldn't you keep this? Maybe I'll buy her from you if you don't want her. Would be an interesting new way to get to work."

Harbrinder looked back and smiled. "Maybe so," was all he said.

Five minutes later, they were approaching Richardson Bay. Katherine was surprised to see the *Blackfish* isolated on the edge of the channel. Even her untrained eye could see how strongly the current was ebbing out the Golden Gate and pulling on the *Blackfish's* anchor rode. It looked like she was anchored in a river instead of the Bay.

Harbrinder positioned the tender directly against the overhanging stern quarter of the *Blackfish*. He kept the propeller in gear and quickly tied off a line before cutting the motor.

"Wait here while I open her up." Harbrinder pulled himself onto the *Blackfish* without looking back at Katherine. He unlocked the companionway and dropped below.

Katherine stayed in the tender and watched the current go past. It would be an awkward climb up the stern of the *Blackfish* by herself. She was willing to wait for a helping hand.

She heard Harbrinder moving around down below and scrambling back on deck. Smiling, he said, "All set, let me help you aboard."

Katherine didn't hide the wary look on her face, but she reached up for Harbrinder's hand all the same. Was this going to be a good surprise or quickly become awkward?

She followed Harbrinder down the companionway stairs. She couldn't see much with him in the way, but there was a smell. "Stuffy" wouldn't quite describe it. "Stale" was closer, but with some medicinal undertones. Then Harbrinder stepped to the side, and she saw they were not alone. She stared for a second, her eyes not registering what she was seeing. It seemed impossibly out of context as two separate worlds collided in her consciousness. But there was a pale, sickly looking version of Michael lying down on Harbrinder's sailboat. She rushed over, dropped to her knees, and shook his shoulder.

"Michael! Michael! Are you okay? Michael!"

"Oh you recognize him? Yes, he's fine," Harbrinder said. "He'll be sleeping a little longer."

"Where did you find him? He's been missing since yesterday. We need to call the police."

"You can call the police later if you want. First I need to show you what Michael and the Ethics Committee have been doing."

Katherine looked up at Harbrinder, processed what he said, and then looked back at Michael. The top of her scalp started tingling, and she felt suddenly nauseated. What had Harbrinder done? She realized Harbrinder must have brought Michael out here. And did what to him? Still on her knees, she reached over to make sure Michael was breathing.

"Michael will be fine, Katherine, trust me. On the other hand, what Michael, your company, and the Ethics Committee have been doing is not. This goes way beyond an argument about consumerism or news media. This is the systematic manipulation of most of the planet."

Katherine kept looking down and tried to stay calm. She was suddenly very aware of her situation. She was alone on a boat with Harbrinder. What she didn't know was where he was going with this, what he knew about her involvement, and just how crazy he was.

"Let me show you."

Katherine flinched slightly as Harbrinder leaned over to help her up and position her to view a glass with Michael's face on it. He started the video, and Katherine watched as Michael, clearly under duress, answered questions about the Ethics Committee and Level 0 embeds.

Katherine didn't know all the details of Level 0 embeds. She didn't want to know. But she'd known they had existed for years. Peter let her in after the incident in Costa Rica. She never had an issue with it. She trusted Peter implicitly. The world was going in a bad direction before Artemis and had since come to a better place. That was just a fact. She watched the video, but her mind was focused on the man standing next to her. Was he showing this to educate her or incriminate her? Was she about to end up like Michael? Katherine stood very still as Harbrinder leaned in to inject the occasional comment. "Been going on for years." "Stealing people's free will."

The video ended, and Katherine stared silently down at the cabin sole. She didn't say a word but was legitimately shocked. Harbrinder apparently misread the cause of her distress.

"Incredible, isn't it? I know this is a lot to take in. You've been working for this company for years, but I want you to know I don't blame you. You've been used by them as well. Doesn't that upset you? It upsets me. Not just that they've been manipulating the general population, but they have been personally using you. Well, guess what? Now we have a chance to strike back for all of humanity."

Katherine looked up at Harbrinder. *My god, he assumed she didn't know.* Even now, he thought the pretty comms lady was an idiot. The condescending asshole.

"Katherine, I have tickets booked tonight for Hawaii. It'll look like two lovers getting away for the weekend. From there, we'll make our way to Hong Kong, where we'll be safe. We will be the heroes of our generation."

She still didn't say anything as she looked back down.

"I have these recordings of Michael confessing. Digitally water-marked and indisputable. Beyond that, look what I found." Harbrinder pulled out the Safety Glass server. "I'm sure they'll be able to get the data off of this in Hong Kong."

Harbrinder stepped over to Katherine and took her by the shoulders. "Finally, Katherine, we have you. A high-ranking employee at Artemis who has come over to the cause of freedom. You will inspire so many people, Katherine."

Katherine turned away from Harbrinder. She needed a minute to think.

"Katherine, I know you must be overwhelmed, but I want you to know I have your back. You don't have to worry about anything. I have plenty of money overseas, and we can transfer your accounts over the weekend. We'll be fine financially."

Katherine stayed silent.

"And I know you like to work. There will be as much of that as you want. Taking down Artemis will be a full-time job. Or, if you prefer, you can help me work on OpenCast. I have several companies in that space."

Katherine looked up, turned, and stared at Harbrinder. "You have several companies working on OpenCast?"

"Yeah, you bet. And I think they will be very busy, very soon."

Katherine quickly turned back around before Harbrinder could see how angry she was. He never mentioned he was working on OpenCast. She thought back to how they met. How he was always asking questions about her work. About the Ethics Committee. The lying piece of shit. She had been used. She glanced back over at Michael. That was her fault. This was all her fault. Then she looked straight ahead at the navigation station in front of her.

Harbrinder noticed the glance toward Michael and said, "Don't worry about him. Despite his crimes, he'll live. I'm no murderer. We'll put in an anonymous tip as soon as we're in the air to Hong Kong. He'll make it through a day in bed."

Katherine's attention stayed on the navigation station. She thought back to flirting with Harbrinder down below her first time on the *Blackfish*. She sat at that chart table asking what everything did, playing up the silly girl act men seemed to enjoy. There were electrical switches and navigation displays. The chart table opened up, and she asked about the paper charts, calipers, pencils, and the large sheathed rigging knife inside. Harbrinder had said, "You always keep a sharp knife handy on a boat to cut a line in an emergency."

Katherine stayed silent with her back turned to him. She sensed Harbrinder's weight shifting from one foot to the other, growing impatient. She could hear his hand fiddling with something in his pocket.

"Katherine, you haven't said much. What are you thinking? Do you think we can do this together? I hope so."

Katherine looked at the chart table. She thought about the knife. She thought about the data Harbrinder had. The impact it would have on the world. The impact on Peter. Then she turned around, looked Harbrinder directly in the eyes, and said, "I think . . . I think we have to do it, don't we?"

"Yes! Yes, Katherine, we do. And we will."

Harbrinder took his hand out of his pocket, reached over, and embraced Katherine. Then she pulled back slightly and said, "You promise Michael will be okay?"

"Yes, truly, he's just sleeping. Admittedly with some help, but just sleeping. However, we'll want to be far away from here before he wakes up. We better get going."

Harbrinder led the way out of the companionway into the cockpit. Katherine followed behind, eyes darting from side to side.

"What about the *Blackfish*?"

Harbrinder stepped outside the lifelines and onto the overhanging stern. He bent over to grab the line to the tender. With his back to Katherine, he started to say, "It's a shame, but . . ." when she pushed him from behind as hard as she could.

Harbrinder tumbled into the water, fully dressed and without a life jacket. The current grabbed him, and he was well behind the tender before he surfaced.

Katherine could see the look of shock and anger on Harbrinder's face as he struggled to swim back to the *Blackfish*. She searched for something to protect herself with and grabbed a winch handle. Looking up again, she saw it wasn't necessary. Harbrinder had given up fighting the current and was being swept toward Sausalito. His head was still above water, and he was less than a mile from land, but she had no idea if he could make it.

She thought about what to do next. She was nauseous, and her hands were shaking as she brought out her glass. No signal. Fuck. Harbrinder must have an EM shield. She went back to the navigation station and turned off all the switches on the electrical panel. Still no signal. Then she looked down underneath the chart table and saw a big red knob at her knees that said 1, 2, Both, and Off. It was on 2. She turned it to Off. She heard some beeping, and then the *Blackfish* went silent. Her glass had a signal again. She started to dial 911 and then paused. If the police came, what would happen to all the data from the Ethics Committee that was still on board? Would it end up going public? Maybe she should call Peter first and ask his advice? But, from a legal perspective, she didn't want to drag him into this. If this did end up in court, how would it look if she first called her boss instead of the authorities? It would look like a cover-up, that's what it would look like. But at the same time, she actually needed to cover this up.

She sighed, took a deep breath, and then called someone she hoped would make it all go away. She called Jack Price. The little shit.

"Katherine? This is an unexpected pleasure. Why are you calling me on a Friday night?"

"Jack, shut the fuck up. I found Michael Sullivan, and I need your people over here."

"Wait, you found Michael Sullivan? How?"

"Again, I need you to shut the fuck up. There are complications associated with the Ethics Committee. I need your people here first, before the police. Understand?"

"Looks like you're on the water. Is that right?"

"Yes," Katherine replied as she noted how quickly Jack could track her location. The little fucking shit.

"Okay, we'll have a team there shortly."

Katherine's hands were still shaking as she sat down on the bunk across from Michael. She thought about Harbrinder and broke out in a cold sweat. She needed to get out of there. She scrambled up on deck to throw up over the side of the *Blackfish*.

Looking up and wiping the side of her mouth, she saw the fog spilling in over the Golden Gate, shrouding the sunset behind. The cold air pushing into Richardson Bay chilled the sweat on her forehead. She scanned the water for any sign of Harbrinder. Nothing. She collapsed onto the cockpit seat, her mind still racing. How long would it take for someone to come? Jack's branch of the government probably didn't do much work on the water.

Ten minutes passed, and still no one approached the boat. She decided to risk a text to Peter. *"Found Michael. He's alive. More to come."*

Peter & Linda

P eter was pacing back and forth in the living room.

"Come on, Linda. We're going to be late."

"We're fine, Peter. They aren't going to run out of sushi."

Peter smiled to himself. She was right, of course. He was just anxious to have some fun. They were finally going to get together with Sandra. Dinner at the sushi place in Alameda they used to haunt, and then Sandra promised to take them bar hopping in Oakland. A Friday night like normal people. He was looking forward to more of that.

Linda walked into the room. "There. I'm ready, old man. Let's eat."

"You look beautiful, my dear."

"Yes, I do," Linda said with a smile as they walked out the door toward the multi-rotor pad.

Peter's glass buzzed on the walk over. It only did that for a few people, so he stole a look. It was Katherine.

"Everything okay?" Linda asked.

"Yes, in fact, things just got better. Katherine says they found Michael alive."

"Really? Where? What happened?"

"No details. Just says more to come. Anyway, he's alive, and that's the important thing. I'm sure Katherine will send more info when she has it," Peter said with a smile.

Jacob was waiting for them at the pad.

"Good evening, Mr. Graham, Mrs. Ngo."

"Good evening, Jacob. Think we can go to the west tonight?"

"Absolutely, Mr. Graham."

As they stepped into the multi-rotor, Linda teased Peter. "I thought you were in a hurry?"

"In a hurry to be with you. Besides, the sun is setting. It will be worth it to go this way."

The multi-rotor took off, banked over Racoon Strait, and passed Belvedere Island. If he looked down just then, Peter would have seen a Coast Guard fast response boat approaching a sailboat on the edge of Richardson Bay. But Peter's attention was on Linda's hand in his and the sun just peaking in under the fog before it finally set.

They turned southeast toward Alcatraz and saw the city lights starting to glimmer in front of them.

"You were right, Peter," Linda said, squeezing his hand. "It was worth it."

A minute later, they were passing between Treasure Island and the City. The multi-rotor lurched forward, accelerated hard, and dropped to just a hundred feet above the water.

Linda gasped and squeezed Peter's hand harder.

"Jacob, what are you doing?" Peter shouted.

"I can't . . ." was all Jacob said before they slammed into the mid-span tower of the Bay Bridge, utterly destroyed and sinking into the water below.